In a

Blue Moon

Catching up with the neighbors...

Jon W. Shaw

In a Blue Moon

Indy published - Jon W. Shaw

ISBN: 9798690414023

4

In a Blue Moon

Other stories by Jon W. Shaw:

<u>Annotated Notes in Time</u>

Book 1.   <u>EARTHS</u> ©
Invisible Presence

Book 2.   <u>LINGERING EARTHS</u> ©
A Precipitous Presence

Book 3.   <u>ENDURING EARTHS</u>©
A Propitious Presence

-STEMMING TROUBLE©
Adventure

Due 2020-21:

<u>In A Blue Moon</u>©
Adventure

<u>Serendipity</u>
2021- Growing up

Players

Wyatt Cantu - Astrophysicist
Alouette Cantu - Chemist
Perla - Astrochemistry
Richard - Physics
Auch - (ouch) Moon Man
Proxy – Auch's wife
Zonies – Floating robots
Maud – Floating robot helper
Tart – Another floating robot helper
Ambassador Boxer - unlikeable sort
Carter – Investigator
Sophie –Office manager
Sparky, Rute and Sim – Zeta Reticulin
family

Locations

Lono – Moon underground city
Zeta Reticuli – 39.8 lightyears away
82 Eridani – Satellite planet in Zeta Reticuli
Alpha Centauri – 4.34 lightyears away
Proxima C – satellite planet in Alpha
Centauri

Dedicated to my
Impossible girls

Elizabeth, Katy ,Olivia

Chapter Chart

Chapter Chart

.

Prologue

Wyatt, at the end of a long day on the keyboard was finishing the final changes on a talk he was going the give to the Cal Sate Astrophysicists Department. Thinking he was almost finished, he let himself wander into another thought and found himself arguing with himself… again.

"This here and now we know and are comfortable with, has evolve mathematically into so many different perceptions of realities with endless possibilities. The Space between Space holds a paradox, an enigma. The focus on the very small instead of the vastness of the observed elegant Universe is the key."

Noting, that's a weird place to finish, hum, maybe I'll change that, I suppose I gotta stop somewhere.

Lightheartedly, talking to the air on his way to make some new coffee, finding it helpful to verbally run through the high points of a talk he would be giving soon.

"Wonder when I should add the possibility of off world enhancement of human DNA to the mix? When would be an appropriate time to add that in any presentation?"

Getting the coffee machine satisfied, he had someone on his mind. Taking a quick scan of the pool visible in the front yard, then stepping outside into the side yard and a sultry desert evening that lent itself to what greeted him. Lounging under a ramada with her new read 'Stemming Trouble' was Alouette, a cheveux noirs beauty,

"Hy… tired of thinking?"

"I do believe you have hit the rail on its head, as my Dad used to say…"

Alouette "Your father commanded a better vocabulary. than that, don't you think?"

"Hum... you are vary correct. You look perfectly comfortable with the evening, I'm making some coffee, want some?"

Eyeing him over the top of her pad, with a little bit of an exaggerated look of astonishment,

"Absolutely not! There's a bunch of other fun things to sip along with this evening of the day. We've got some chardonnay chilling, these sunsets merit a better trimming than coffee, don't ya agree..."

Setting her things down with A quick smile, she slipped off to get what was suggested. He warmly reflected at the happen-chance surrounding Alouette, he never felt the need to question the allure she still had on him. Years ago at collage, as she drifted across his field of vision he felt a sudden accord. Of course, having an attractive mysterious look about her naturality didn't hurt either. After some embarrassing attempts at introductions, they got together and found themselves talking and loving into the silence of the early morning hours, sometimes with pause enough to hear a solo dove cooing out on the terrace. Amazed to find that she also had a mutual unexplained prescient attraction to him. They both were interested in likewise oriented majors and uncovered some other parallels in kind. They found a love for the desert, so much so, that she had helped him build this small getaway here in Borrego Springs years ago.

Wyatt sat back absorbing the lingering strands of indigo and burnt/raw sienna that kindly tinted the departing light. Still, his talk was lightly nagging, so he rambled on a little more,

"With our future's inevitable advancing technology, we will find an answer, as a whole we may not agree with.

Becoming aware of a manufactured reality that through no choose of ours, we play our parts in. How many different dimensions will there end up being…"?

Wyatt had a solid understanding of how things mathematically work together with what he was speaking about. Even still, he found this particular theocratical neighborhood so, so way out there. It would be a brutal joke to except the idea that all our reality is for someone's or something's experiment. Or at the extreme maximum, for someone's amusement.

Offhandedly hearing the electric corkscrew toil as it passed into the cork, then 'Pop,' clinking of two glasses.

Alouette, lightly sliding back in her seat, bringing with her a lingering aura of fresh air-conditioned environment from inside, of course that just furthered her mystique. Constantly adding a fresh angle without a hint of effort. She easily brought him out of his swirl of thought.

"Perfect idea, perfect timing, as you perfectly do most all things…"

Small kiss,

"Thank you, I think, hum, you are pleasantly plump with prosperously perfect pronouns this evening. How do I follow that up?"

Wyatt "You Just did without even trying... As for me, I tire of the lash of the overlord."

"Well then, now how about doing something tomorrow that involves exercise! Instead of the two of us sitting around writing most of the day."

"Ok, what are you thinking: riding, hiking or flying?"

Alou "I was thinking of heading over the hill to Mt. Palomar."

Wyatt sitting back, and feeling the need to get his mind off what he had been working on,

"You know, it's been a while since I've hiked or packed anything that far, I don't think we'd be up for that. Although, you do carry everything so well, not too much extra anything in all the right places. But I know your intention was for another purpose of sum-sorts, and I'm taking up space & just filling air."

Alou taking his hand,

"It's so nice of you to still charm me after these years...thank you. Yeah, I got an email from Perla, you know her from my side of the office.

She's got a boyfriend, you met him, that is doing a study of the Moon, guess there's more o2 up there than the Space agency is telling us. That has me interested in the chem stuff, and she has something else she wanted to show us. What's ya think?"

"Heck yeah, sounds great, I might still know people up there, I spent some time at Palomar when I was doing my graduate material. Cool, we can stay in the bunkhouse and watch stuff all night! But where do you have the hiking come in?"

"Well, we leave here in the morning, an hour later we're there, take a picnic and hike a little bit amongst the trees. There are tree up around the top isn't there?"

"Yes of course, that sounds just right."

With the calendar of events for tomorrow settled, they moved over to a floating settee to better accommodate their views of the lingering layered sunset. No words for the moment, content to be just side by side, hand in hand.

Chapter 1

A bright warm desert morning found them on a two-lane road coming up on Warner Hot Springs. Wyatt was asking Alouette if she had ever been in,

"Yeah, Mom & Dad used to take us on the weekends several times, I kinda liked it. You ever get a chance?"

"No, I tried but they required a membership commitment."

"Now that you mention it, that might be one of the things that piqued my interest in chemistry."

Wyatt "How could that be, just a thermal pool isn't it?"

"Sort of, actually there were two large pools, one cool and one hot. The obvious thing that caught as kids was the aroma. Especially during summer mornings and evenings, very heavy Sulphur, probably smell it if we roll down the windows."

Doing that, they were awarded with what was forecasted as they drove by.

"There it is. First thing in the morning, my brother and I would walk back to the source of the spring along these little fenced trails. Most every time we walked back there, we would meet a very old looking Indian chief, at least that's what he said he was. He told us to drink the hot water from here every day. There was always a long-handled ladle and a stack of cone shaped cups, if we did, we would live to be as old as him."

"That's a nice little story, yeah my nose gets it. So, the smell of Sulphur brought you to the halls of higher learning. Remind me to tell that to our kids one day."

Lightly grabbing his driving arm,

"Oh, do you mean it! I was just thinking about that last night! Let's start now!"

"Here, right here! You want us to pull over and do it right here? You have to get off the pill first…"

Alou "Of course! don't be silly…"

Wyatt "Well…of course if you would like to find a spot for a blanket…"

"Ok, ok, ok well later, we have been together for five years, and I've been thinking a little more about children lately. No, we can wait a little for a more propitious time."

Wyatt "Dad would be so happy your using his phrases. It is, I guess, about time to consider more of our future, I want to think together."

Just passing the Glider port,

Alou "Hay look, someone's going up, you want to reserve a sailplane for tomorrow when we come back by?"

"So much to think about, kids, flying and who knows what we're going to find on the Moon tonight…You make our life out to be kinda busy, is there any time for a family!"

Alouette "Ha-ha, I think we will be perfectly fine. Yeah, lets. I'll call you drive. We can argue who will be pilot in command tomorrow."

They both loved to fly, and so, reservations were made for the following early afternoon.

For now, enjoying the slow winding road as they threaded their way up the mountain, each was silently absorbed with the different possibilities of their future.

18

Finding the lot empty, they parked anywhere they wanted, walking up to what appeared to be a deserted observatory.

Ramp and steps, knocking on the side door (round building) after some moments, they were enthusiastically welcomed in,

"Hay, you made it!"

"Hi Perla! Gee, what's it been 2 weeks?"

"Ha, yeah about that, hi Wyatt, you guys having a nice vaca?"

"Yep, we've had a slow very nice time. You have Alouette and I interested with the moon and o2?"

"Well, two things: what we fell into is so far-out, I think the two of you are just what the doctor ordered. Seams there's a lot of stuff that just doesn't agree with what we've all been told. Get in here and let me amaze you two!"

For Wyatt this was all familiar, Alouette was new here, so she was the one asking questions of her hostess.

"We brought along sleeping stuff and a bunch of food, so we won't' be a bother…"

"Oh, you shouldn't have, I thought Wyatt spent some time here and would remember the bunk house and the kitchen, all that stuff is always still available."

Wyatt "I mentioned that, but we decided to be safe and bring some things. We were thinking about a little walk out along the ridge later, why don't you guys come along?"

"You gotta see this first."

Making their way around to the computer console with multiple displays, she landed on one.

"Check this out, the Lunar Atmospheric Composition meter read outs from Apollo 17. It's still working but look at the first set of numbers it sent back in 1972. And now look at the latest group."

Wyatt "How are you getting that frequency, I thought the Gov. had all that stuff locked up."

"Well, I could tell you but then I'd have to make you do dishes for a month! Later on that, look at the difference! The Surface Boundary Layer is eight times thicker now!"

Alou was now looking at the chemical make-up from the filtered spectrum telescope that measures percentages of Potassium, Sodium and other trace elements.

"Look at the difference of these two percentages, which aren't found on Earth, Mars or Venus, but I've seen these on Neptune, Jupiter and Saturn."

Wyatt, speaking very comfortably,

"That's because the Moon was towed into orbit from one of the adjoining Moons of Saturn."

They both stopped what they were doing and looked at him,

"WHAT?!"

Perla, half joking "Have you guys been drinking?"

Wyatt "I'll tell you all about it, you two haven't heard this? The very early Greeks and Persians wrote about a night sky with no Moon...No? Later then."

Alou, looking at Wyatt with a scrunched-up nose and a questioning face,

"Forget that, look at the Helium levels and the o2 percentages. If we just put on a filter for various other noxious gasses we could walk around up there in t-shirts!"

Wyatt with a confidant smile,

"Hum... I know for a fact that you are, very thankfully, not that thick skinned..."

"Oh, you know what I mean, so who knows about all this? Just you guys here or is the Government in on this too."

"Yeah they are on it. Right into the ground if we let anything out, no joke you know, we end up in super max lock up. So really, don't tell anybody.

Sorry, but I had to tell somebody, and that's not even the real beginning to this story…"

Wyatt "Are you kidding, I love it!"

Alouette "I'm kinda fascinated myself."

"Ha-ha, I knew I called the right people."

The small banter went on for a time, then Wyatt brought them back to what Perla had brought up earlier,

"Hay, you mentioned some other thing about the beginning of something…"

Perla pausing herself, taking a deep breath, then exhaling,

"Hay-ok-wow… I'm gonna let Richard tell you about the particulars of this next one. Come on…"

Following along down a set of stairs to the basement, finding a small side hallway with four doors leading off.

Perla "This one may take some getting use too…"

In the sweep of opening the locked door, a slight ozone odder was present. Stepping into an expansive dim workshop, Perla flicked the lights on, what visually met them was most confounding for their world as they understood it. It demanded their attention: a fifteen-foot-high x fifty-foot disk, silently floating one foot off the floor. Very off worldly looking and exactly like what you'd expect, if you knew what to expect!

Wyatt "Find this on a Mission Valley used car lot? Holy Shit!"

"We sort of bumped into this…um, wow…guy… hum. Richard is shopping with our new friend at the moment, so they can explain it best. All I really know is, this is from the backside of the Moon! And so is the guy.

Alou "I'm gonna sound really silly, is he three feet tall?"

Perla answered flatly with a direct look,

"About our size, but different. You'll know he's not from around here."

"Like four arms and antennas?"

"Oh, now come on Al, too much Hollywood in your diet. No, just exaggerated almond shaped eyes. To be honest at first, it's creepy, but you get used to it, he wears a kinda sunglass."

Wyatt was off surveying the craft and halfheartedly heard what was being said, offhand yelling from the far side of the machine,

"Where's the door?"

"It's over here."

Following the seamless curvature of the craft around and stopping where he started, astounded he stated,

"He's got the key's… This is the most incredible engineering I've ever seen! No seams!"

Alou softly amazed,

"I wasn't even thinking of that, I'm kinda lost with it floating off the ground and there's no sound!"

Wyatt "Well, there is that but push on it… it moves at the touch of a finger!"

They stared at the astounding stillness for a time, we humans, being so use to things that function to produce a noise. This was a reactionless flying/hovering craft!

Perla broke the silence after a minute,

"The guy needed a metallurgist to combine some different metals for parts for a machine up there, so he came down and asked Richard. Apparently, the Moon is lacking some key elements. The story goes, they met when Richard used to ride motorcycles around Ocotillo Wells, down by your place. Over the years Richard somehow kept their meetings quiet even with me, occasionally they would meet for the same kind of things as this trip. This is the first time I've met Auch."

Al "Auch?"

Perla "Yeah, like I poke you real hard and you say…"

Al "Ouch! Easy enough for me."

Wyatt "The Government isn't all over this with you guys in jail and this craft over in S-4 being taken apart?"

Perla "I wasn't kidding when I was talking about super max lock up!"

Wyatt "Now hold it, you said…"

Perla "Ok, I was just talking about the Government knowing about all the extra air up there. No way, no how do they know anything about Auch and this craft. We would be in some lock down for the rest of our lives, that's if we were lucky!"

Wyatt "I know for a fact, that would be a fact. When I first got into Astrophysics years ago, the military would be overly interested with anybody that would report anything to do with ETV's. I learned fast to just enjoy the sightings and keep quiet."

Chapter 2

Wyatt talked the girls into a little ridge walk with a late lunch along the backbone of the mountain. The cloudless early afternoon was refreshing, after the heat of the desert and the intensity of the morning disclosures.

Wyatt "Figured we have time until Richard gets back, Perla you said 4:00?"

"Yeah, this feels good to get out, we don't do enough of it, at least Richard and I."

The trail was wide enough to walk abreast and do some catching up for 20 or so minutes. Wyatt was quiet for a while, Alouette had some new questions,

"I was thinking about how you got involved with Richard and this whole deal, and since you work at our company this is really going to bring our business into an association with what's happening here by default."

At this, Perla stopped on the trail and very purposely took hold of the conversation,

"Working for you guys is extremally important to me. I understand if you would like to disassociate completely from these two projects here and that if you would like me to take myself out of your business, I will. What Richard somehow stumbled on, is making everything else pale in association. I didn't know how to tell you Al, I thought the only way was to let you guys see what's here so you would understand my decision."

Wyatt "Thank you for your consideration and concern, I think this looks like a Hallmark picnic spot. Would you like Pastrami, or Turkey?"

Perla, looking between Alouette, then Wyatt for a few seconds then,

"I'm very serious, I don't want to quit."

Al "Help me spread the blanket, you aren't quitting anything, I was merely being an opportunist, I hope you don't mind…partner…"

Perla, in a small mental dust storm that quickly cleared,

"You two are punks! You already talked about all this while you were out at the car!"

Al "Ha-ha really do hope you don't mind, we were talking about how much we love San Diego, but wouldn't it be nice if we got a cabin in the woods?!"

Wyatt "Well we were kinda tossing things around like kids, cabin's and flying saucers…"

Perla "Wow, kids!? They'll make more gravity than Element-115 can offset! Don't get me wrong, I love em!"

It was a whole different world with the crisp mountain air, adding in the occasional Steller Blue jay's letting everyone know just how right where they were. A light breeze through the branches of Douglas Fir and the White Pine was offering up the sound of flying and Perla remembered it,

"The gentle wind through the trees reminds me of flying with you Al along time ago, Wyatt you gotta take Richard gliding I know he'd love it. Oh, and thanks for the Sammy & chips, just right."

They thought it best to ask the real questions regarding the hardware and the visitor when Richard returned.

Ending the picnic/hike found them walking through the parking lot, Perla seeing Richard's truck,

"Hay look, they beat us back. I know I don't need to say this but be as normal as possible please..."

Alou "Oh come on mother, we're all grown-up here... sorta. All you have to do is politely stop me if I am asking to many questions."

Perla "Fair enough, let's go."

Unlocking the door again, they found the lights on, and the door of the craft open. Perla walked up to the door, leaning in, she announced,

"Hi you guys, we're back."

Richard "Hi you, we be out in a minuet."

They all tried to busy themselves with other things until Richard and Auch stepped off the craft.

"Wyatt, Alouette, fantastic to see you both! This is Auch. He is visiting us from the Moon. It seems that they needed some different metal elements from our Earth to finish a project they were working on."

Wyatt "A very distinct honor to meet you Auch, is it customary to shake hands?"

"Yes of course, we are not that dissimilar from your Earth here."

"My name is Wyatt, and this is Alouette."

A small time of mild uneasiness passed quickly, just seeing him answered a lot of internal questions for both newcomers.

Auch "Come on a tour, you will find there's not a lot to actually see. We don't travel far in this model; it is what you might call a work truck."

As they stepped on only to see; a short hallway, then a round central room with seats and a small control desk. Wyatt had a thought,

"A question, is the source of your anti-gravity Element 115, or at least that's how our periodic table identifies it?"

"Yes, the same."

Richard turning to Wyatt "How about I bring you up on all that stuff later, Auch wants to get going with what he came for."

Auch "I'll be happy to give you a working tour at another time."

So, gratefully they stepped off and watched. The basement of the observatory required a short freight tunnel for large equipment for the telescope. That, in combination with being on the slop of a ridge, lent itself to a natural entry/exit along the slope of the mountain.

The Craft, with some minor electrical ionizations around the base left a flat ozone tint in the air, very quietly started moving out of the open tunnel. The group followed the slow movement and paused at the tunnel mouth.

The electrical discharge stopped as it lifted farther away from the ground. They watch it silently, slowly float up through the trees. Once above the trees, it turned on its side, then moved away so fast, you could almost say it disappeared!

After all the appropriate wow's and jaw drops, it was decided on the slow thoughtful walk up the tunnel to retire to the forest view deck.

It was a favorite sunset hangout for the staff and itinerate Dir.'s here almost on the top of the mountain.

Perla "White or red?"

Alouette "Chardonnay is really all I care for."

Wyatt, again with a little playful boy humor,

"I knew there was someone else!"

"Ha-ha yes you caught me... in so many ways-(kiss)"

Getting settled on the deck with warm overcoats on, toasting each other to staying out of trouble.

That reminded Richard of a situation that he wanted to get absolved, so he dove into a problematic explanation.

" Ok Perla, I wanted to tell you this with someone present-(Grabbing her hand)

Perla, I know you thought I was seeing someone else, but I was on the Moon! Several times, for days... This is finally over; it's been killing me cause I knew you had concerns."

She held him level in her gaze, with a mildly surprised expression,

"You are sorta right... at first I started to think along those lines. Then I came to my senses.

You couldn't possibility be with anyone else; cause I am the finest there is! And soo Hot!"

Perla had everybody laughing very hard, Alouette almost lost a swallow of wine...

A little farther on, all thing settled into Science of the Ship.

"Alright, that craft is indescribable! It has no electrical wires! For the most part, he thinks his way through space, there is a central room with some fixed chairs you saw, a small control board that only he can see when the craft is operational. As it moves, it warps space in front of the craft and falls into it!"

Wyatt "I was under the impression that Fiber Optics played a large part."

Rich "He actually let me see the; main reactor above, the three gravity amplifiers on the floor and the three emitters under the floor. I've never seen anything out of place, it's like it's a conscious robot so far as I can tell, but we can ask him about that next time.

Perla "Ok flyboy, remind me why, when Auch took off just now; why his brains weren't pressed together against a wall in the opposite direction of flight due to the acceleration of the craft...how many times have you gone to the Moon now?"

"I don't remember, each time it seems like the first to me. I do know that the gravity reactor generates a heart shaped field around the entire craft at start up. That simulates a one-G environment around the entire craft making the people inside continuously experience that same one-G. Even in the high-speed abrupt turns...that's why."

Chapter 3

The following morning at breakfast had the newcomers were making new plans,

Wyatt "Hay you know, would you call and cancel the sailplane before we get too deep?"

"Already done while you were in the shower."

Richard "Don't change all your plans just for us. We are in no hurry."

Perla "You could take me again Alou, we could leave these guys here so they can do whatever they do...it's not that far away. You haven't' taken me up in a long time..."

"Hum, well since you apparently are the best girl in the world, I guess that's the least I can do!"

Everybody chuckling, phone calls were made again, all things were back on.

So, the girls were off on their way winding down the hill to the glider port.

The guys were also on their way, but they just didn't know it yet. As they were finishing the dishes, Richard got a call on his iPad.

"Hay, we are going to have a visitor, forget this for now follow me!"

Running down the stairs, unlocking the lab room door and turning a switch, the role up door started to wind up.

As they stood there watching,
A round floating saucer silently came to a stop right in front of where they were standing. For Richard this was nothing new, for Wyatt...Wow

Silently a door slid open and Auch stepped out.

"Hello so soon, I need the other section of machinery. Am I interrupting something?"

Richard "Welcome Auch, absolutely not, let's go grab it. Do you have your gravity stick?"

"Yes, I have it. Would you both like to come along?"

Wyatt knew he was looking at him, but he still asked,

"Me?"

"Yes."

"Yes!"

Trying to be a casual as possible, he followed the two around a bench or two, then stopped in front of a large crate. Auch placed what looked like an oversized heavy tv remote on top of the box. Pushed a group of inputs, standing back, the crate lifted off the floor one foot! It was floating! He and Richard easily guided the wooden box to the threshold of the craft.

At that point, Auch entered another set of numbers and the box lifted to one foot above the interior floor height of the craft.

Auch "Would the others like to be included?"

Richard "Not this time, they went gliding, they'll be out for the day. Wyatt do you want to give Alou a call?"

"Your funny Richard, 'Hay sweetheart I'm going to the Moon, be back for dinner. No... Oh, um, but are we out for a long time?"

Auch "We can drop this off and come right back. Any time you would like."

Entering the craft, Wyatt was stunned into a temporary silence.

"Yes, I think I'll just sit over there, or you tell me."

Richard laughing,

"You see Auch, it wasn't just me acting like this..."

Auch, motioning "Sit in this seat."

The door had closed at some point, and even before he sat down, he noticed a very slight lateral movement. Richard was telling him,

"They have no use for seatbelts. All you will feel when we accelerate to speed, is a one gee pull in the opposite direction of travel. It will take about three minutes to reach the spaceport. This is really great! I finally have another human to relate to! All this time and I had to keep quiet about all this. Wow, I can't wait to have Perla see all this. Speaking of unbelievable! You ain't seen nothing yet!"

In the time Richard was explaining everything, Auch had turned on a view screen. Wyatt watched the craft approaching the dark side, and as they started to slide towards the side of a large crater lights were lit. A very large complex along the shadowed lip came into view. Being a pilot, the small row lights reminded him of an instrument approach.

"How many times have you had the pleasure of seeing all this?"

Richard "I can't remember, I really don't know. But I still get the same thrill as I did the first time!"

Arriving at what appeared to be a waterfall, it was explained later that it is a 'liquid plasma airlock.''

Once inside, a large clear convex door slid back into place. Their ship came to rest on the floor next to at least 12 - 18 distinctly different categories of vehicles.

"I know there's questions but let us unload and you just follow along for a time. Ok?"

Wyatt was quietly nodding in agreement and smiling. As they moved the crate out of the doorway, the surrounding complex looked entirely astonishing!

32

The complex had very few outwardly exposed structural elements, mostly along the shadowed side of the crater. That wasn't what required his attention at the moment, the vast arched underground was so incredibly expansive!

Wyatt felt a little in the way, so stepping off the craft and off the side. He suddenly, realized he was breathing air, and the temperature was approximant as what he was in ten minutes ago. Ten minutes ago! Oh my God! I was on Earth!

He was thinking all this and didn't hear Richard trying to get his attention.

"Hay Mr. Wyatt! Come with me for a few."

Dutifully he fell into line and followed. Walking back towards their entry port, he visually locked on to a very long curved clear ceramic observation area. Finding a cluster of lounging furniture, they sat down, or at least Richard sat down.

Wyatt finding himself drawn to the 'window' formed along the crater wall, standing and staring.

"You can ask questions now, I'll bet you haven't noticed something very important yet."

Wyatt "Oh I think I've noticed a lot!"

Pulling himself away from the view,

"I love the desert and that's what I always thought the Moon was like. Seeing it now, I am having a tough time quantifying it. It is, but it's not."

"I'm gonna bet you still haven't noticed the big picture yet."

Sitting down and looking at Richard for the first time,

"Ok, fill me in on the bigger picture."

"You saw the different vehicles and the landscape, but you don't see the different people."

Turning his attention from the window, to people clustered around other tables or standing in line, he now slowly survey the others around him. It hit him like another ton of bricks!

"Oh, man in Heaven…"

Chapter 4

Cheerfully engaging the many turns and twisting's of the road down to the glider port, out over the desert some cumulous clouds were starting to form. Perla was asking whether they would help or hinder their flying time.

"We are gonna need some around to help with lift, and it helps me see where that lift is going to be. It's really a lot of fun, I'll let you fly some if you like."

Arriving at the glider port, Alou and Wyatt had done a lot of flying there at the FBO, (Fixed Base Operators, Start Shack) so they were being towed by a Rockwell Thrush commander (retired crop duster) along the runway before they knew it. Speaking with headsets/mic. Alou was giving a commentary of upcoming events,

"We're dropping off a little higher this morning due to the lack of heat off the ground, so we might need to do some circling up with the tow plane.

Once we get up to 2000 AGL I disengage the tow line. What do you think?"

"I forgot how nice all this is!"

"Yeah, I like it-we like it, it's fun when Wyatt and I fly, he thinks it's better over there, I think it's better here. We go back en forth trying and we usually end up somewhere else along the way getting all the best lift!"

"I don't have a pilot's license; do I need one?"

"Well, aircraft are all different, all the aerodynamics change when there's nothing pulling or pushing. You kinda have to use your brain to make it fly. You don't need a single engine pilot's license, but you do need a sailplane license."

The small talk ended when Alou pulled the disconnect, and a small pop sounded.

"Now we are flying! Ok, I think over along that ridge that leads up to the observatory is going to be a good one to follow for a while."

Perla "It's beautiful today! Well, at least out over the desert. Back towards town looks a little smoggy. How high is the observatory, remind me."

"It's about 5,600 ASL, we are at 7,600 ASL now".

[ASL= Above sea level]

"I think I see it on the gage here. The observatory looks so small…. Woo Look at that!"

An ETV appeared flying right along beside their glider, it appeared to be one like they had seen in the basement of the observatory.

"WOW!"

"That looks like Auch!"

That issued from both girls, it then slowly peeled off down towards the observatory on the far side of the ridge.

"Auch must be coming back for something, that still is really incredible!"

Alou put the plane into a shallow bank and started circling directly over a few times. A few moments later, the two boys were out in the parking lot waving at them. Perla got on her phone and gave Richard a call,

"Hi from up here! We gotta do this you an me! We just saw Auch, did he forget something?"

"Hello to you too! Yeah, he needed that last crate. You girls fly safe, you look great up there! Have fun!"

"We are! See ya!"

36

Al "That's too bad, those poor guys stuck on the ground, o-well. We are going to avoid the clouds that are starting up over on the desert side, so I'm going to break away from the top of the mountain. We'll fly back along the ridge for a while."

"You know, maybe Wyatt could take Richard up sometime. He hasn't done anything like this for a long time…"

Chapter 5

It's safe to say, Wyatt truly was having a challenging time placing all of this in a reasonable order of rationality. Taking Richard's que, he refocused from the external view of the Moon crater, to the interior and its inhabitance, he had to mentally steady himself once more. The everyday movement of some of the individuals of course was natural to the individual, but not at all natural too Wyatt.

"I, I think I'll think on this for a while."

He found a bench to land on.

"If it's too weird, we can go back to the ship..."

Truly, the thought crossed his mind as he panned the communal area. But his inquisitive empirical scientific mind won out.

"How many different civilizations are we looking at..."

"Well, on the last count in the known universe, one hundred seventy-three, but here only maybe four."

Still slowly studying the diverse groups of 'people' not lingering to long on any one group.

"I think I have a lot of apologies to make to a lot of people."

"You ok Wyatt?"

"Yeah, I mean I've been looking in all these people's back yard without their permission for years."

"Ha-ha good! I thought I lost you there for a minute, hay, we gotta get back, I see Auch heading back to the ship."

Getting back on board, Auch was explaining,

"I am short with time. Next trip, I'll take you for a tour."

That was all the talk for the moment, setting themselves, all things started happening in reverse order.

The view ports were all on, and as they passed through the collimated particle beam door, it was like passing through a sparkling waterfall! He hadn't noticed it the first time, this time Auch left the forward view screen on. He could see the Earth rush at him! Along the way back, Richard had a thought,

"Hay Auch, Perla is flying with Alouette around the mountain. Think we could spot them on reentry?"

"Yes."

It was thirty seconds later; all the view ports came back on. They were floating three hundred feet off their wing tip!

That had the two guys just as shocked as the girls were.

One of the view ports had a close up of the two girls in the cockpit, pointing and smiling, they appeared to recognize the craft. Still with big smiles and waving, they slowly moved away, and Auch maneuvered the craft into the waiting tunnel. Moving things along, Wyatt thanked his host.

"Thank you, Richard, thank you Wyatt, until next time. This is for the other two."

He handed a folder to Wyatt, and the two stepped off the craft. It immediately started to float out of the tunnel.

Wyatt took one look at the file,

"Hay come on, let's go take some pictures from the ground of the girls if they are still circling!"

Running up the stairs out the door then down the stairs, finding them still circling in a comfortable wide flat circle.

Wyatt shouting, waving "You won't believe where we just were!"

Richard 's phone started ringing and I think you know what was said.

Chapter 6

"This must be contained, not even the smallest bit of information can get to the public. And what about those people still at the sight, we closed that whole place a month ago.'

"They have been warned and reminded of the consequences. There are only two people on sight for maintenance purposes.' There are no other support staff permitted."

Chapter 7

The Day of flying was celebrated with B-B-Q steaks and veggies, plus an abundance of champagne!

This evenings feast location was just on the inside area off the deck. The clouds had covered the treetops in the area, so it made for a warmer talk inside. Wyatt and Richard were encouraging the girls to tell them all about their flying daytrip before telling them about their jaunt to the Moon.

Alou "It was the oddest thing, Auch suddenly was three hundred feet off my wing tip for some minutes. Then floated away, it was amazing!"

It was at that moment Wyatt couldn't wait to bring up the Moon trip, he very casually handed Alouette a folder.

"Check this out."

All conversation trailed off a little,

"Oh my God!"

Perla couldn't stand it, she leaned over to look-an-see,

"Oh my God again! That's a great shot of you Al, I don't look so good, kinda air sick..."

"No you don't, you look fantastic. My hair looks like a scared black cat on Halloween! That was nice of Auch to go out of his way."

The two girls were kinda lost in the fun of the picture.

The two guys were smiling at each other, Richard kinda swished his hand fast over his head, and the two started laughing.

Perla "What's soo funny? Hay, how bout smore champagne!"

Alou "That would be nice, look at that profile of the glider, it's beautiful."

Letting the girls talk, the guys went about their business, cleared some dishes and holding back smirk's. Richard couldn't stand it,

"Aren't you gonna ask how we have those pictures?"

The two smiling ladies were happily contented with not being serious for a time,

Perla "Sure, the Man in the Moon gave them to you when he dropped in. The Man dropped in from the MOON! Ha… And by the way, he is much more handsomer in real life, than that picture of him up on the Moon! Ha-ha…"

That did it for everyone, nobody could contain themselves, they all lost it!

Chapter 8

Waving good-bye to a gratifying weekend, Wyatt & Alouette headed back to Borrego Springs. Alou was running some thoughts down the mental highway about what to do with the information. An esoteric avenue possibly, they had all this new knowledge and only a hand full of people she could make a case with it.

Where would she go with it in the first place, all she could think of was the end result = trouble.

A few hours later, finding themselves sitting on the two-person gliding settee again, watching another evening awash with color, comfortably again with each other.

"If you and I put a study together to project a future of o2 acceleration, who would benefit? I just don't want to do it for exercise."

The revelation of Wyatt's trip to the inside of the Moon would bringing a clash of historically indicated attitude, they have their freedom and their business to consider.

Wyatt "I can only see a future of being overrun by the government if we publish anything about this. I know they now have all the information on the Moon people. They obviously aren't doing business with the Moon, or Auch wouldn't have to go through Richard for parts. I wonder if they are even interested in us humans. I also know we are regarded as too violent to be included in even the lowest class of sentient life from the Galaxy's point of view."

Alou "That is a fact, maybe they don't want us around at all."

Wyatt "I got it! Why don't we change the game, let's ask Auch if they have a counsel of the Galaxy or neighborhood watch, something like that.

Possibly ask if we could be included as ambassadors to the forum from the Planet Earth!"

There they let that thought linger in the air, much like the festive colors in the evening sky. A brief questioning thought followed along from Alouette.

"No offence, but how do you know they have a 'United Planets' like our United Nation's or ha-ha a 'neighborhood watch'....ha-ha."

"Ha- it's all I could think of at the moment, but there must be. When dealing with large numbers of anything there's a requisite type of hierarchy.

And to strengthen my position; if the Government knows about the Moon, that means the military is involved. That can only lead to the obvious. You and I have witnessed way too much history in our brief lifetime and it almost always turns out bad for the everyday guy.

So, what do you say..."?

Alou "That might work, once we introduce ourselves on the Moon, our people can't do anything to us. If our people try and remove us, hopefully that would evolve into a lot of questions from the people on the Moon....Hum..."

"Of course, that might get us in way over our heads on our 'everyday jobs.' I think it would be worth it."

The determined talk went on into the evening, dinner was put on hold for subsequent glasses of wine. That lead to action,

Wyatt had Richard on the phone.

"Why didn't I think of that…You know that's a really good idea! This had to be Alouette's idea, your too out there!"

"Well, I do have some bright moments, and so far, I'm pleased with this one."

All things went into motion, Richard was first to take the idea to Auch for review and wait for an answer. They had established a communication link quite a while ago, a device given to Richard that resembled an iPad.

Alouette and Wyatt thought that whole idea would take weeks of deliberation on the part of the representatives of the Moon and beyond.

So, they turned to picking at some dinner and packing, closing the desert home and ready themselves for work over in San Diego on Monday. Phone again,

Richard "When can you two leave."

That was all he said.

"Ah, excuse me. I didn't get that."

"Auch was extremely open to the suggestion and wants you to meet with a sub-council. Is it just you or are you thinking of the two of you?"

"You know what, I gotta call you back, give us ten minutes, bye."

The phone already perked Alouette's attention. Wyatt turned away from the phone,

"Hay au… they want to talk to me."

Alou "They who?"

"On the Moon…they."

"Oh Me Gee! Me too?"

"Well, it was my idea, so if you don't want to…."

"Are you fucking nuts! Of course I'm going!"

"Ha-ha you said 'fuck,' ha-ha, I've only heard you say that a hand full of times! You must think this is important!"

A little loving banter back and forth between the two, Wyatt called Richard back.

"I guess Ide like to introduce the two ambassadors from Earth, Alouette and Wyatt Cantu."

"You guys know you just jumped a freight train going 80 miles an hour, you sure?"

At that, Alou made her presence known,

"We will be up after we finish closeting up here."

At that she turned and dug right into what was needed. Wyatt hung up and did likewise, making arrangements with his sectary in San Diego.

It wasn't ten minutes later all things changed: New instructions from Auch and from Richard regarding the departure point.

Chapter 9

An hour later, Richard and Perla, just cruising off the grade into Borrego Springs. Perla was bouncing things back and forth as to what part if any they wanted to get involved with.

"This can be a watershed moment in the history of the human race! It could go bad if regular people like us aren't there to put our voice in. So, I love you, but I'm going to go with Al."

"And you think you're getting away from me that easy. Well, you really don't know me quite yet do you. Do I have to remind you that I held a secret for two years, and I introduced you to my friend Auch?! Hum…"

"I know! It's going to be so much different fun! I can hardly wait. Ok, here we are."

"So, you were just playing with me… again…"

Turning into the desert home of Wyatt and Alouette, they were met in the car port with considerable excitement.

Alou and Perla were hugging like they hadn't' seen each other in a year, Richard and Wyatt had big smiles on their faces as they were watching the girls. Moving inside, they each wanted to find out what the other had to offer.

Richard "I was thinking that if we are gone for a time, someone will come up to see how things are moving along on the o2 front. If you two would have driven up that would be two cars in the garage. That's two too many. Before we left, we both went over the place for anything that remotely connected us with the Moon."

Wyatt "That makes perfect sense, so what's the plan for us meeting up with Auch?"

"Tonight at 1:00."

Alou "1:00 where?"

"Here."

Needless to say, the preparations got a little hectic.

The three that hadn't spent the night on the Moon before had questions on questions. Richard was very patient and reassuring. What he did do was sit everyone down and explain the nature of the inhabitance and their quirky nature. He did have pictures to help with the explanation.

"There is another thing that I bet Wyatt didn't really pick up on, it's the different smells. Some are actually sweet smelling, and without a doubt, the inverse is also true.

Try and be as polite as possible, also there are translators that are worn around your neck with an ear plug. Obviously, the air is sanitized and purified, the majority of inhabitance are o2 breathing. The others that are not, must support themselves in whatever way that makes themselves contained."

Perla "How long are we staying, do you have an idea?"

"The longest I ever stayed was five of our Earth days. I have no idea on this one, but I'll imagen a couple of days."

Alou "Well, let's put that all down for a moment, all we have here is stuff for spaghetti/no meatballs. Or we could go out, what would we like to do?"

It was unanimous. They landed in their favorite Mexican restaurant just off the circle.

Still talking in quiet tones and starting to really feel the weight of what they all hoped to accomplish.

This wasn't just another meeting. This was going to be the entire world talking through them

No one was remotely tired as each one furtively scrutinized the clock every ten minutes. The three acres of desert

48

the home sat on was ample room for Auch's craft to set down. At the appointed time, Richard received a call on the pad.

"Ok, let's go."

Locking the side French doors, heading out into a seemingly empty night in the desert.

Richard was the one with preceding experience with identifying a veiled Extra-Terrestrial Vehicle. He'd almost ridden his motorcycle into one years ago at night when he first met Auch. He approached a blurry soundless shimmer, a perfectly outlined sloped door appeared floating one foot off the sand.

He paused and assisted the others on board. They found Auch in the central room, helping each one to their seats. As soon as Richard entered, he turned and sat down and the door closed.

Auch "Before we leave, I'll say that you have taken a considerable steep. I will help you in every way that is available to me. Do you now have all the items you will need for personal comfort for seven of your days?"

Yes, was the collective answer. With that, he turned to face forward, putting his hands on a seemingly empty shelf, all of a sudden, the view ports all came on.

Ten seconds later they all felt a small one gee tug in the opposite direction of travel they witnessed on the view screens. As they watched, the Earth was scaling down in size on one view screen then on another, the moon was filling the view screen logarithmically... fast in another!

The screens abruptly went dim, a crater side wall was approaching, then what looked like a waterfall came into view. Passing through that, all the screens went dark. Ten seconds later

the craft door slid open and the interior of the Moon was
revealed and waiting for them, they had arrived in Lono City.

Chapter 10

Auch stepped out to assist his guests disembark, he was paying attention to the ladies to brace any possible inner ear reaction.

"Richard has previously been here and knows the details, I'll let him see you get settled at you sleeping areas. Then we will take a small tour of the facilities. Richard I'll pick all of you up in 30 minutes."

Turning away, he left them in Richard 's capable hands.

Alou and Perla were astonishingly quiet.

Richard "Come on let's get a golf cart, at least that's what I call them, I can't pronounce the name they give them here. It's a longer trip from here to the apartment that it is from Earth to Here!"

Normally that would have gotten a few laugh's, but not even a nervous chuckle at the moment. Walking over to a group of 'golf carts' that were floating one foot off the floor. Silently moving along a wide arch hallway, much like an airport here on Earth. A sweeping view out into the crater on one side and kiosks' and branching tunnels on the other. Passing what looked like a food court and some shops that suspiciously looked like tourist traps.

Rich then drove onto a large elevator that lifted two flights. Then moving on out toward the clear ceramic window along the rim wall they stopped in what could only be called a garage, but with the nicest view!

"All right, this is home sweet home for a while. Grab your stuff and get ready for another mind wipe."

Opening the door with a thumb print reader, Richard casually called out:

"Hello Maud!"

Five seconds later, a floating robot that looked like a ten-pound coffee tin with arms and a small head appaired.

"These are my friends, and this is Perla the girl I told you about. I'll get her settled in my room, could you show Wyatt and Alouette to their room. Don't forget you guys, we have to meet Auch in ten minutes by our front door, ok?"

"No sweat, be right back."

In a very pleasant female voice,

"You are correct Richard; she is very beautiful.   Wyatt please follow me,"

Bonjour et Bienvenue Alouette Puis-je vous aider?

"No thank you, I have it. You know my language?"

"Yes, French is just one of the two hundred eighty-seven languages I translate."

Silently they moved along a short hallway, then stopped at another door with no hardware.

"Each of you place your thumbs on the rectangle, that will be your key. Follow me please."

Floating into a very nice room with a view that was nonstop Moon and semi dark Space beyond! Maud gave them a short tour and then left. Wyatt was staring at Alouette, and she was giving it right back!

"Oh Me Gee! Wyatt do you realize we are on the Moon! The Moon that the people who lived in caves could only look at! And fifty years ago, it took three days to get here. It took us three minutes!"

Alou sat down on the edge of the bed, trying to assimilate everything. How can any of this be.

Everything she knew had just changed in three minutes! All of what she saw everyday was made by some people's decisions to keep the peoples of the earth buying what they sold. Here was a place where it seemed, there were no boundaries.

Wyatt "Alouette, it is a lot, I understand how you are feeling right now. You want to stay here and settle?"

Slowly looking at everything, and then to Wyatt,

"No, no I don't think so. I'll kick it off and ok, let's get going."

Perla was expressing the same emotion, except she had an additional wonder,

"How did you ever, how could you, why did you keep all this to yourself!"

"I thought it important. I thought you more important, I didn't want you to think I was nuts..."

Perla "Look out there! That's the Moon!"

"You ain't seen nothing yet! Come on!"

Auch had driven a larger 'G-cart' to accommodate the group. Their first stop was the communal area, there he explained the only thing they need for any services was a thumb print. Then it was on to new territory for all.

Auch "I would like to introduce you to the 'United Galaxies' or your 'United Nations.' The attendance arrangement is not similar at all. All the ambassadors from outlying areas are as you will see, on viewing screens located all around the meeting area. The local delegates will be seated with you in this hall here."

They exited the vehicle and entered a large chamber.

Richard "This looks like our House of Representatives, but bigger sorta. How often do you hold sway?"

Auch "One week, every eight of your weeks."

Richard with an understanding smile,

"I'm gonna bet this room is going to be very active soon."
"Yes, in fifteen of your Earth hours."
That brought a little surprise to each of their faces.
Alou "How are we to prepare for this assembly?"
Auch "You have a syllabus in your rooms. My intention was to show where you will gather, for now relax, and have some time to look at the video on the pad. I'll take you back to the refreshment area, and please walk back to your living rooms."
Richard "Oh yeah, I forgot to tell you, their big on exercise up here. They almost have Earth gravity here, almost. You probably haven't' noticed it yet."
Wyatt "Yeah I kinda feel lighter on my feet, but nothing like the first astronauts did. That's ok with me, I've been sitting to long anyway. Ok, what's for lunch."
Richard was trying to explain the menu to each question.
"It's all kinda good, they have an Earth section on the menu, so a cheeseburger looks like one, but no way does it taste like one of Wyatt's B-B-Q one's."
"Thanks man, well let's see how this goes, I'm kinda hungry. Alou, Perla how are you two coming along?"
Perla "I'm sort-of here, how about something bracing to drink? Anything Richard?"
"Oh man, their version of a martini is really "Out of this world!"
Alou "Yes please!"
Their first dinner as ambassadors actually went very well. The walk back along the crater rim looking out into the stars was unforgettable.

Chapter 11

According to the video intro, it really wasn't much different that formal proceedings on Earth. At the appropriate hour, the new diplomats were met by Auch and driven to the event. He added a few words that hadn't occurred to them for some reason.

"You will be seated next to two other representatives from Earth. They are not so pleasant."

Wyatt "I knew the G-men would somehow squirrel their way in. Must we appear together or is it everyone independent on their views?"

"You should state your views as you see them. That is why I was very pleased with your offer. Take these interpreter lanyards and headphones Ambassadors."

They were shown to their seats by one of the floating A.I.- icons and were introduced to an extremally out of sorts Ambassador Boxer.

"Who are these people and how did they get here! They are not representatives of Earth."

The robot stated flatly,

"They are welcome here and will be recognized as equals. You will have no further comment."

With that said, the robot turned to assist other people or beings.

But the Ambassador was still spiting bullets,

Wyatt "I'd listen to the coffee can if I were you. Wouldn't it be a shame if they had to censor your group."

Not really knowing how things work here, he decided to take the chair next to their new colleague.

That upset him all the more, and he let them know that. Wyatt ignored the protests, purposely turning to his group,

"Look what we got ourselves into. I'm just gonna let him run his mouth and let the folks here see what they are dealing with."

The 'Come to order' was called by a person that was quite a bit different than your everyday human being, parts of the head were spikey! It seemed that no matter what part of the galaxy you might be from, fundamentally, all large gatherings of respective bodies function about the same.

New business was called for and Richard, Perla, Alouette and Wyatt were introduced. All the screens erupted with applause for five seconds then abruptly stopped. That had all the kids from Earth thinking about 'canned laughs.'

And so, the day carried on with breaks every two hours. Some delegates mentioned local concerns, others were grateful for support others had rendered. When it came to Earth, the Ambassador stood up and with abundant vigor, protested the new additions.

"These four delegates have not been cleared by our Pentagon or White House! I'll not have unelected or unapproved delegates representing our Earth!"

The Speaker of the meeting ask a question.

"How is it that you are present here?"

Richard stood up,

"Mr. Speaker, my good friend Auch has placed us here to…"

"Say no more, you and your delegates are welcome. Let me remind this gathering, all are welcome here.

All are welcome to leave as well. There are no guidelines regarding qualification. If we need to remind a certain delegate... Ambassador... there is another less courteous alternative. Next business..."

At the end of the day the Ambassador had to make his presence known.

"I intend to take this back to the Pentagon and the Hill. I'll find you out however you found your way here!"

Richard evenly and direct,

'Well, here you go your ass holiness, just to save taxpayer dollars. I've known Auch for three years now and he and I have been making regular trips. Seems to me he wouldn't have recommended us if things were working out here as they should. Any physical or financial harm that comes to any of us will be brought up here in this forum. Is that UNDERSTOOD."

The boiling and popping Ambassador turned and pushed his lieutenant out of the way, as he stormed off.

Richard turned to his group,

"And that's how you do it on the Moon!"

The four broke out with a sizeable laugh that caught the attention of some of the other departing delegates that made them smile. Or it the very least, it appeared that they were smiling.

Chapter 12

Very deep (Ha-ha) self-important people were just arriving at the observatory. As they seem to do, they drag 8 black Suburban's along. It's no wonder they can't pay their employ's well.

They were planning a 'quite approach.'

These fellows - (good-for-nothing, reprobate, wrongdoer, evil-doer, picaro, scumbag, pig, swine, louse, hound, cur, rat, beast, son of a bitch, SOB, low life, skunk, nasty piece of work, ratbag, wrong 'un, git, toe rag, scrota, spa peen, sleeves, fink, rat fink, butthole, scamp, dingo, cad, heel, rotter, bounder, bad egg)- all dressed alike, had the same sniper sunglasses the same everything. What always tops it off, the same blank expression. They spend so much time with their finger in their ear, or fondling their weapons, talking on the telephones, making sure they don't shoot each other or themselves.

Ok, ok, on with the shit show. Of course, nobody had a key or a way to pick the lock, of course they brought along a battering ram so they could 'sneak- up' on the support staff. Then once in, they all quickly spread out with everybody making hand signs, as if the 'quite' battering ram didn't already wake the dead! And again, everybody had their gun out creeping around corners, with both arms outstretched like they were holding dirty dippers and looking for the t-can.

Wait for it, wait, here comes,

"Location secure, combatants have escaped."

58

How in the hell did they jump from two people who were maintaining the observatory to 'Combatants?'

And then two guys sniffed around inside while ten others 'Agents' stood around outside talking about …

This shit drives me crazy!

Chapter 13

The newly appointed diplomats decided to celebrate their appointment with an extravagant dinner.

Perla "Hay Hun, do they have any expensive restaurants here?"

Richard "Sure do, I've already made reservations. I would like to show you a little more of this place on the way."

They of course walked and were introduced to the most unusual elevator they had ever seen.

Wyatt "It's a large transparent tube, with an opaque floor and no buttons to push. Wow. How does it work?"

Richard gave it his best shot at an explanation as they stepped on and appeared to ascend about sixty feet.

"I don't know…"

Arriving in a short hallway that led to a dome with a clear ceiling, suddenly above them was all Space! It gave you the feeling of standing outside on the Moon!

Alouette "Oh Me Gee! Look at Earth!"

They all were mesmerized. The Amber color of the Moons atmosphere gave the stars and earth a subdued finished look, but that didn't matter!

Richard let them gawk at the unparalleled scene while entering his name on a floating pad. A fancy floating coffee tin located their table. Getting settled, Perla offered,

"Richard, I'll change places with you in a little bit so you can get the Earth view."

"That's very nice of you, but this whole floor rotates, so we all have a slowly changing view of our Solar System."

60

Over the course on the evening, they had to remind themselves that they would be going back to Earth and the everyday jobs soon. The evening was really very nice, and they did have a wonderful time. The other dinging patrons' appearances were vastly diversified to say the least, but they were very literally looking past all that!

All the serving staff was robotic, silently always ready to serve. They lingered long with dessert, in all truth, it was for the view.

Walking arm in arm back to their suite, they were met by Auch, giving them a schedule of the following day events and a question.

"Do you have any comments or questions?"

No, was the unanimous response, and each passed on their way. The group decided to stop for a night cap along the rim viewing bar.

Wyatt "I was going to ask Auch about any observation equipment they might have here. Have any idea Richard?"

"Man do they ever! They all like to keep their eye on Black holes, asteroids and meteors. With domes like the one we were just under, there are the obvious reasons. I'm not quite sure how many there are scattered around."

Alouette "So let's go back to what Perla's research was saying: what's up with all the o2 all of a sudden, is someone manufacturing it, or is it propagating naturally?"

Richard "I don't know. Since you two are the Chemists, I think you should ask Auch.

In fact, remind me to ask him for a tour of the mining operations for all of us."

During the finish of the week-long session the verbal confrontations between the Ambassador and the four waxed and waned like the tide. The Speaker, by the end of the week finally added with a weary tone, that this was his second warning.

Auch had agreed to tour with them the day after the assembly was completed. So today the delegates all piled in the floating golf cart and then stopped at a tram station.

Auch "We will look into the mining operations out towards the North"

Stepping in the group found themselves in a wide tunnel with occasional tunnels branching off.

They passed small talking points back and forth for about ten minutes, then coming to rest at another crowded station. It wasn't the kind of crowd the earthlings would expect, the total make-up of the group was robotic!

Auch "We will stay here until they move off to their assigned locations."

A few minutes later had them walking along a hallway that had quite a few doors leading to who knows where. Auch approached a door, slid open, walked right into another large room with open golf carts.

Slowly moving along a clear tube, he pointed out separate phases of the mining process. Also, what distinct types of mineral and quantiles that is exported.

Alouette and Perla of course had Chem questions, at that Auch launched into an explanation,

"The difference in core composition and the fact that the moon is almost a billion years older that the Earth. The mineral composition of rocks found on the surface of the moon varies drastically from those found on Earth. The abundance of titanium is one example of such an anomaly, with certain lunar samples containing up to 10 percent of this very precious mineral. The highest abundance of titanium on Earth has never exceeded 1 percent.

Here there are some others: mica, brass, radioactive elements like Uranium-236 and Neptunium, some of which are found naturally on Earth. The moon itself was brought into orbit from Neptune, which has other larger moons..."

That rightfully impressed the group, but naturally they were all blown away with the news regarding the origin of the Moon, all but Wyatt, and all he could say was,

"I stand corrected."

Everybody looked at him with questioning faces.

"And what I meant was, I suggested the Moon was from around Saturn, Auch has corrected me. It's from Neptune."

They all quietly decided not to question Auch directly right now. Actually, they were stunned into silence.

After a brief time, Perla wanted to ask about the o2 spike here. Auch responded with,

"It is with mixed feelings that the outside atmosphere be enriched. Your Ambassador is leading that effort, there are some others that are interested in populating the surface."

Wyatt "Establish a stratosphere and thermosphere! I wonder why so close to Earth?"

Perla "Why would that be an issue?"

"Well, if a large meteorite hits the Earth, the physical effect of the possibility of orbit disruption, spin rate or at worst, dislodge substantial portions of the mantel. That would leave the stable orbit of the moon in question. My understanding of colonization it to further the Human species."

Auch "Those are possibility's, but what I and others are concerned regarding the military is: a platform to establish fixed locations to launch attacks into Space from."

That humbled and maddened the four. Understanding that we Earthlings are ready to fight at the drop of a hat over nothing. Why we can't change it, is lunacy all too itself.

Wyatt decided to change the subject,

"How about we step away from that one and move on into the optics available here."

Auch "Yes I assumed you would ask. That is our next stop. Telescopes similar to what you are familiar with are still in limited use. Most of what is used now carries a 'Quantum' platform. What you are now experimenting with, the Quantum computers as you call them. Ours carry a sentient aspect that takes the guess work out, as you would say."

They had moved away from the mining operation and were now in another clear tube that moved the vehicle along quite fast.

No, there was no wind in the face and hair flying, just the feeling of fast. Maybe three minutes passed then slowing and moving away from the tube to park.

"Here we will take a few moments to look at what you might call the weather station and the airport. They monitor any incoming meteorites or excise dust. They also take care of all the incoming and outgoing traffic."

Stepping into a large room that, in all appearances, was a cross between an observatory and an airport control tower. There were four 'people' at various stations, and no one took notice of the visitors. Auch explained that,

"Your Earth telescopes have higher resolution than anything we have here. If something is of interest some large distance off, we easily go there."

Wyatt "Why of course! Why didn't I think of that! I was kinda hopping for a thousand-inch mirror that could see its tale! Well that does make sense."

Auch "It does make things easier with observation. We have a universal rule regarding assisting early evolving civilianization's. All base science must originate and be contrived on Earth. This includes all chemical compounds or improvised variations. Perla and Alouette, you are welcome to our library, any amalgamations you find you can use.

But all the elements must be found on earth or obtained from space by only the means available on Earth. In other words, your private space mining companies."

Alouette "Wow, I'll look into that next time we are here, that is, are we invited back for the next session?"

"Most assuredly. We enjoyed the way you handle your Ambassador. You would say we laughed."

That gave the new delegates heart.

Chapter 14

Stepping off their craft in the quite of the early desert morning, and watching the blurry outline disappear. Unlocking the side door, stepping in and letting their stuff hit the floor, throwing themselves at a chair or the couch to rest. Quietly staring at nothing, listing to the hum in their ears, each one reviewing what just happened.

Wyatt "I have a good feeling that our regular work is going to be kinda boring."

Richard "Ya think!?"

That lightened up the room a bit.

"Wyatt do you have anything like what we like to drink around here, I really don't care for Tequila at the moment..."

"Asking the wrong guy, ask the girl."

"Coming right up."

She and Wyatt stood up at the same time. She headed for the kitchen, which was part of the living room. Wyatt stopped and just looked at things, something was off. He could tell. When a person builds a home, that person knows when things have been moved. Slowly moving through the other rooms, then returning. He went to the desk and scribbled something on a piece of paper.

Walking around naturally, he let each one read the message. Grabbing the glasses and went outside, away from all the structures. Alouette was most worried, whispering,

"What's going on??"

"There's been people here, and we all know who that means the Ambassador and his playmates.

I'm sure they sprinkled the place with bugs, Richard you know a little about it, would it include video too?"

"Did you find any?"

"No, I can tell each room is different than when we left it."

Richard "Well how about this, let's act as if we thought the Ambassador was an ok guy, not overboard. And let's keep Auch out of things as much as possible ok?"

They all were sorta weirded out, especially Alouette.

"Those assholes were in my house!"

"Ha-ha that's my girl… don't worry we'll do something about it. Be patient."

Entering and carrying on as if nothing was of interest,

Richard "Well, I for one am glad we have tomorrow before workday.'

Perla "You mean today."

They all chuckled

Alouette "Then stay till tonight and head back up Monday morning, we can have a swim and a hike today."

Perla "I like it!"

And so, the early morning went, with the sun coming up the warmth had them all in the pool before they knew it.

Wyatt "Isn't it terrible, it's too warm to take a hike shoot…"

Alouette "That was laden with so much sarcasm, I'm surprised you don't sink."

Monday morning came early for everybody. Richard & Perla headed up to Mt. Palomar, Wyatt & Alouette headed back to their South Mission beach house.

Alouette, stepping onto her bayside deck, reaching for her keys- seeing the door ajar glanced into the disheveled living room and stopped.

"Wyatt those cockroaches have been here too!"

He came around quickly,

"Don't go in. I'm calling the cops."

Alou sat herself down on a deck chair and started to call her work. Her plan was to start back at work on Wednesday, but she wanted to see if anyone had been asking for her. She was told that some federal agents had removed her computer and searched her files.

"Hay Wyatt, you better call your office, the Feds took my computer and some other things!"

"Alright I think this means we are going on the offensive. I'm calling Richard."

They both were sitting on their deck that is bordering the bayside boardwalk. Both now in a funk, waiting for the police in quite review. Not paying any attention to the summertime skaters and bike riders happily passing by right in front of them.

Wyatt's Phone started ringing,

"Wyatt, the observatory was broken into and we are in jail, call your attorney and explain to him that we were with you guys camping this last week."

"We were broken into here at the house, I think it's time we ask Auch for some help. Is there any way I can get in touch?"

"They have confiscated my pad, but there is another way, but I don't want to tell you on this line."

They exchanged numbers for their legal representatives and made plans to meet. Wyatt called both attorneys and started the bail and release process.

Chapter 15

'Well, look what we have here!"

Ambassador Boxer seemed to be pleased with what he had confiscated. He tried to open it with his thumb print, but no results. He then handed it to his Tec. people.

"Take it apart, find out how it works. Call me as soon as you find something."

Unbeknown to him, was the fact that the instant he tried to open the pad, that opened a channel directly to Auch. While he was ordering it taken apart, Auch sent a command to 'Melt.' And it did. Before their eyes, it silently slowly turned into a pool of plastic on the table.

I'm sure you can imagine the blood pressure of a certain someone!

While that was moving along, Auch called Wyatt and found him sitting on his deck waiting for the police to show up.

"Auch! We were just trying to figure out how to get in touch. Richard and Perla are in jail, both our homes have been broken into. I am sure I know who the culprit is. Is there any way you might be able to help in any way?"

"Yes. I have informed the Speaker of the Counsel. He has sent a message of no confidence and miss trust, and possible expulsion of the ambassador Boxer. Terms are:

Return of all property, reinstatement of all original transcripts and records. Absolutely no interruption of remunerations and the addition of some.

70

All records of this act carried out on you four will be destroyed. All records shall reflect Ambassador Boxer as having been severally reprimanded.

The removal of all visual and audio recording and any such device being reinstalled in the future will not be tolerated.

All actions will be completed within twelve of you Earth hours.

No further retaliatory action will be accepted.

That will return You, Alouette, Richard and Perla to your normal operating states."

"Auch, we thank you so much, one moment, Alouette is taking the phone.... Auch you are my hearo! I overheard everything! Thank you so very much!"

"You are welcome. The police will not be responding to your call. A team of carpenters and cleaners will arrive instead. I'll drop off two more pads for the four of you to use. Tonight, at ten o'clock by the volleyball court in front of your home."

"Thank you we will be there!"

Just then, down the alley came four service trucks, people pilled out and went right to work.

Of course, Alouette wanted to direct the crew cleaning, and since Wyatt built this home, he also put in his two cents with the carpenters.

About an hour later a limo pulled up and out stepped Richard and Perla, a catering company followed them.

Richard "This is the most roundabout way I've ever come to the beach, but I really like the end result."

Perla "Do you guys have an extra room here? I want to move in!"

This all had started about 10:30 in the morning, and now was 4:30 when all the service crews were done. They had moved into the dining room that looks out over mission bay and were sipping complimentary champagne and watching the colored lights getting long across the water.

Richard "I have some questions for Auch, I know you guys probably have a few things too. And I know he won't want to linger long right outside here, so why don't we write our questions on different papers and just hand them to him."

Close to Ten o'clock, they all headed out to the far side of the v-ball court. As they approached, the blurry outline of a large craft became evident, an invisible sloping door slid open and there stood Auch two feet above the sand!

"Good evening, I hope all is much better, here are the two pads. I cannot linger."

Richard handed him an envelope and they all together, "Thank you Auch!"

With what looked like a smile, he turned, and the door closed. Small coronal discharge sparks for two or three seconds, then they could feel the void of its presence silently gone.

Chapter 16

Well it seems Mr. Boxer was not really taking his rebuff very seriously. He and his people were now conjuring up other ways in which to cause difficulty for his new-found colleagues. He had some very good resources: the military and had a long-time ally in the senate. His was a private space development company and for years had other programs already in service.

All this sounds as if he had accomplished a lot, but there was really no end product to speak of. Not anything really to do with Space, no rockets, no data, nothing really except promoting more opportunities for aggression. That was his true intention, to position his company at the forefront of whatever would be needed to fill in that gap that was created.

Chapter 17

Whoever suggested their regular jobs were going to pale into insignificance was 100% correct. Richard was the only one that was still kinda close to the action, being back at the Observatory.

His first job was to try and make some semblance of the mess after the search of the offices. Then oversee the re-installation of the copper clad double doors that had been demolished when Boxers group 'snuck in.'

Perla, Alouette and Wyatt were in town at their day jobs and counting the weeks until the convening of the next session.

Alouette "Hay Perla, I don't know how Richard ever kept that secret for almost two years! You know I came close a couple of times on my first day back."

"You aren't the only one."

The weeks did pass quickly, Auch's Pads found their way into their lives a lot more ways than expected. All four were sending questions regarding Science and procedures and how much they could glean of Chemistry/Metallurgy.

It was decided that the Borrego Springs home was secluded enough to launch from. Auch had highlighted the talking points for the next assembly and encouraged any branching speaking issues. There was one other topic he let them know about.

"Your associate, Mr. Boxer is still trying to encourage avenues of aggravation directed at the four of you. Be on your guard and know I'll assist you in any way to offset any trouble."

Alouette sent back a thank you and a request,

"Is it possible to perform experiments in the natural moon gravity without somehow going outside away from the 'Village.'"

He informed her that he would introduce her to a Chem Lab on their return.

Arriving on a mild desert evening with a stillness all around, looking forward to the Mexican dinner in paper bags they were now un-wrapping. Comfortably anticipating their trip to the Moon, passing ideas and far-reaching questions around the table that for now, must stay that way. In and among the talk, the two pads started vibrating at the same time. Richard reached over and looking,

"Looks like our departure time is changing to one hour from now! Auch sez there is line of black cars headed our way in about two hours. He will be here in one hour. Ok well, let's finish what we started here, then put ourselves together."

Perla "That little prick, I'm feeling kinda mean, can we think of a way to jack with him?"

Alouette sarcastically,

"My goodness, did I just hear that come out of your pretty self??"

"Ha-ha yes ok I'll put my smile back on, but that doesn't mean I'm gonna forget it!"

Greeting Auch in the dusk, quickly taking their places with all eyes on the displays, watching the Earth scale down in size and the Moon grow! There was the accompanying one gee force trying to keep them there on Earth as they moved away. While the Moon started to race at them in the opposing view screen unbelievably fast!

Wyatt "Do you know how lucky we are!"

They all smiled, before they knew it, they were passing through the plasma 'waterfall.' Stepping out Auch invited them to breakfast at his suit at 7:00.

On their walk to breakfast, the small company still marveled at all the engineering involved to build this city. Pausing at Auch's door, a thumb print was all that was needed for them to step into a similar living arrangement they were used to here.

"Welcome, shall we sit... I would like to present a possibility. Now that you have seen how things function here, you will notice it is strikingly similar to your order of things on Earth. As you have experienced with your last visit, there are elements within some races that respond with negative intent."

Wyatt "I was hoping that evolvement here would have somewhat marginalized that peculiarity."

Perla "That's too nice of a word for it."

Alouette "That I'll agree with."

"Yes, it has in some groups. In others, the destructive nature is still an underlying influence. Saying that, not everybody you meet here is of like minds as you four. Know to be on your guard for others with disagreements."

Richard "How would we best marginalize any potential large-scale differences, pistols at ten paces?"

"Richard, I know you are jesting. What I'm intending is Mr. Boxer is unfortunately not in a class alone.

There are many planets that have never known war amongst themselves. They only defend themselves against marauding forces."

Alouette "That is truly wonderful to hear. Is it due to education and dedication to Science, or just by nature?"

Auch "You have found both answers. Some come by peace with persistent study with effort. On some planets, the people are born into a peaceful way and have no idea of major conflict."

Al "I have a personal vendetta to settle and I know it's petty, I'll try and keep it under control."

Auch "I am not asking you to cower to any one group or individual. Only firmly but cautiously hold your own."

Wyatt had decided to change things up, this week it was his turn. At the opening He made a point to sit next to Mr. Boxer,

"Well Richard was enjoying you company so much during our last session, I think I'll have a go at it. How are you doing, your G-men follow you along everywhere, or have you recruited some local talent?"

The tall scowling ambassador didn't respond, only moving his chair a small way off.

Alou not so quietly "Now isn't that just what a little boy would do…"

Richard "Let's all be pleasantly diplomatic, please."

The day finished better than it started, with dinner on the 'roof.'

Wyatt "I must apologize for starting the day off on a bad leg."

Alouette "And I was the other one, sorry. I'm very upset that person's goons physically broke into our two homes and we must be polite without taking any civil action against him!"

Richard "Let's be patient, this is only our second week, lets' watch how others react to this person. I'm thinking we aren't the only ones with issues with Boxer."

As a group, they refocused their attention on the incredible display of the Earth, and fanning spray of galaxies of the evening just above their heads.

Chapter 18

And so, the week carried on with some discussions of opening new commerce with planets they were unfamiliar with. Wyatt making a note to ask Auch for clarification on a star map.

The new delegates did learn a lot regarding mining and trade. They also were able to answer some questions from other delegates regarding the same on the planet Earth. They quickly noticed that most of the questions of the day, were now directed towards one of the new delegates. Boxer at times, was struggling to get any attention at all.

Over dinner, the four were trying to establish a way to present the fact of life on other planets. They each were giving thought to the most basic way to disclose the issue to Earth as a whole, this very enormous issue. There are other civilizations that are millions of years ahead of us throughout just our Galaxy. And then the questions of: how can we as a planet adjust our way of doing business and integrate quickly into trade relations, could they aid us, can they aid us? Would they want too?

At the end of the week, Auch knew all these questions were starting to surface. Now that they have had a small amount of experience listening to other delegates, he wanted to introduce the new delegates to another civilization.

Auch "This afternoon, I would like to introduce you to some friends of mine. We will be staying overnight, bring what you require, I'll be by in one hour."

That was all he mentioned, it left the group kind of intrigued on the walk back to their suite. Initially, they had brought suitcases along with extra everything and had essentially 'moved in.'

They were ready and waiting, of course that lead to a lot of speculation on where and how far they would be going.

He soon answered those questions while driving the group to a different part of the complex, a larger hanger with larger craft.

Auch "On the way out, we will be in space two hours, for your comfort this larger craft contains a sleep area, and a comfort room. We will return here in 30 earth hours. Follow along with me and we will get on the way."

As they were walking along the 'space port ramp' amongst larger and very different looking static travel mediums, Richard spoke up,

"What direction are we headed?"

Auch "There are two constellations in your southern night sky we will travel too, Zeta Reticuli Ae. They are a race that has ties to your beginnings as Humans, they seem to 'like' you."

That had Alouette and Perla laughing,

"They found the wrong planet! I don't know how anybody could like all of us here on Earth!"

Perla "Well, I'm really glad they looked passed a lot of things to get us where we are now."

Richard "Me too, am I correct in saying, that's where what we call the 'Gray's' call home?"

Auch "Yes that is correct, they call it home, Zeta Reticulin's, and the other system is Alpha Centauri. Let's get on board."

They found that this ship's interior was arranged about the same as the smaller craft. The central control and passenger space were larger than the first craft. A hallway ring surrounding the central control room, connected to the other accommodations.

"I must stop by some friends in Alpha Centauri first, it will only take a few minutes."

Each one looking at one another with a quizzical expression, finding a seat in the main cabin. Wyatt asked the obvious question that was on everybody's mind,

"If you don't mind Auch, where would that galaxy be?"

As he sat, with response was so daily pedestrian, his hands hovered over certain areas of the luminated control desk without pausing to answer,

"Alpha Centauri. A little over 4 light years at Earth speed".

That was enough to again, have the humans look at each other with astounded eyes and jaws slightly ajar. Their physical presence inside the craft was hard enough to sallow, let alone the distances they were now going to experience. Let's not forget, they were on the moon at the moment.

Rich "Even after a couple of years on these things, I still reach for the safety belt that isn't there. And I still really like the 'waterfall' we go through on the way out."

Auch had the view screens on, as they slowly passing through the plasma interface from o2, out into space. The plasma screen lit-up, sparkling and dancing brightly along the outline of the craft. Slowly moving out into the crater, then pivoting 90°. This time, the view screens went dark, the one gee pull in the opposite direction of travel as usual.

There was a small wring noise that seemed to emanate from the floor, but only for a fleeting time.

Auch "That small sound is from the gravity emitters changing position. It is more pronounced on the larger models of the crafts. The newer versions have that designed out of the system. We should be arriving in 20 minutes, if you would please stay on the craft, the surrounding atmosphere does not get along well with humans."

This temporary destination was quite different from the Moon. The planet, Proxima-b more like an exoplanet. The structure they landed in was just an open platform that retracted 100 feet into the planet surface then a physical roof moved into place. They were unable to see anything except the interior of the large space, they later found out the city was called 'Wethteh.'

Rich "Sounds like a lisping tongue, like Castilian. I wonder if this is where the king of Spain got it from…wonder if the king was from Proxima-b??"

Perla "How do you come up with this stuff, ha-ha… but who knows, you could be right."

Wyatt "It's from riding motorcycles to long in the desert!"

That gave them all a small laugh, Richard couldn't let it go,

"Some of the biggest fun I've ever had!"

Perla "You should go Sailplaning with Wyatt; Al and I had a wonderful time!"

It was about that time that Auch stepped back in and mentioned that on the next trip he would bring along the appropriate breathing devices.

For now, they would be on their way, so he suggested some water or a rest stop before their next thirty minutes. They in turn made the rounds.

Perla "I can tell the facility adjusts to quite a few different body types. That was different!"

Al "yeah, adaptable engineering at its best."

The departure here was not as eventful as the Moon. The platform moved up as the roof slid away, then they ascended 5oo meters, rotated 90° and the view screens went blank with the attending one G- once more. Wyatt had some questions for Auch,

"So, what type of travel are we employing, are we in a 'tunnel' or are we 'warping' space in front of us?"

"This craft does a combination of both, when we go short distances like from Earth to the Moon, we just warp space. Here we add the tunnel to shorten the distance and end result is, most of the time, close to twenty minutes. Here in our traveling today, the most direct routes were not available to both our destination's. Thus, we spend some extra time going out of our way."

Richard "Am I getting this right Auch, the direct tunnels are too full of other travelers, we didn't book our flight soon enough?"

"That may be somewhat true, the tunnels themselves migrate with the changing magnetic fields throughout Space. The availability of the most direct route is never an issue due to 'traffic.' It is the added exit point distance from the intended planet that is what takes additional time."

Alouette "So we have to turn right, left or up, down once we get out of the tunnel?"

Auch "Yes. That would be the closest analogy."

Richard "This is my first trip this deep. I've never gotten 'tubed' before in Space, only surfing."

Perla shaking her head,

"It's a wonder you actually got a PhD. Between all the motorcycles, surfing and skiing, where was the time to graduate?"

"Don't forget the most important part: all the time I've had the pleasure of finding you and is still taking to get to know you."

Alouette "Au, you sound like Wyatt, it's so very nice to have complementary counterparts!"

Both the guys looked at each other with a shrug.

The rest of the passage branched off into speculation on what they might meet on Zeta. Auch's attention to the craft wasn't needed full time, mostly let them carry on only interjecting where and when questions were asked. Richard had a lingering question on his mind,

"Auch, is there any noticeable light inside the 'Tunnel?"

"It is as you see on the view plates, mostly dark with some of the larger magnitude galaxies show as small streaks of momentary light. Our movement via warping the space down in front, and up behind the craft will also distort the light image given off. That is why you will notice the streaks of occasional light are only visible on the left and right view plates. The forward and aft is distorted too radically to allow light to be perceived."

That had the group looking left and right like a tennis match, trying to catch a glimpse of a passing galaxy.

Auch "I am sure that you recall your basic physics: traveling at the speed of light, the observed light is still the same."

Perla "Hold it, please refresh me?"

Richard "Remember when you are traveling at the speed of light, everything doesn't go black. It's like light is going twice as fast, but not really."

Perla "Clear as mud! I remember now, all you had to say is, no matter how fast you are going, light is still coming at you at 186,000 miles a second."

Auch "That is why we see the larger and closer star systems, as light blurs and sometime streaks."

Chapter 19

Setting down amongst another varied collection of craft, in size and shape. According to the view screens, it looked like they were on the open ground in amid surrounding larger structures. Auch had some words before opening the door,

"Here are some rebreathers for you to wear. Have no concern if you do not get a good seal, the air contains higher counts of Helium, so it won't affect you over an abbreviated time.

Remember to 'think' your responses to their questions, it is of course ok to talk they will hear you through the face shield, but they prefer to think. We now will meet with a family of Zeta's and feel free to ask any questions you like."

The planet Serpo hosted a very hot evening sky and three Zeta's (Gray) greeted them as they walked down the ramp. Even before they were close, their thoughts were crowded with "Welcome!" from the locals, and it was weird!

The humans instinctively started verbalizing while still at a distance, each one with something along the lines of,

"Hello, thank you for inviting us, what a nice warm night!"

Auch almost smiled,

"This is the height of the day here, also this tempter is considered hot. We are farther from this solar system's star, which is a Red dwarf that emits more in the way of Gamma rays that translates to radiation = heat."

One of the Serpens added,

"Yes, this is as bright as our sun gets, hence our adaptation in our vision and our diminutive form. We are pleased that you have taken the time to visit our home.

Auch, we would also like to thank you. Let's step inside and sit down, its cooler."

Following along, the earthlings were each a little in shock, everything in the sky above and the Moon? It was larger and farther away, everything was different! The air added more questions to their list. The earthlings quickly found, they needed to adjust their gait, so not to overtake their hosts. That was another question; who was what, Male - Female?? The Serpens were wearing what appeared to be light coveralls covering most of the torso and legs. The fabric was shiny, sort of a soft reflecting finish. There were some subtitle differences: if they were uniforms, gender designation or both.

"We will relate our description of places and people with things you are closely familiar with. Feel free to ask any questions and have no concern regarding your personal thoughts. We do not 'read your mind.' Only anticipate what you might say. It is the easiest way we get whole thoughts out and instruct our machines.

My name is sparky. I am sure Auch has asked you to think your questions, but feel free to speak at any time. I can tell each of you are phrasing questions, so you may start."

Well, the four were honestly overrun with where to start ideas, but it was Richard that voiced first,

"What's your favorite thing to do?"

That had the other three humans looking at Richard with a 'are you nuts?! Look.

"For myself, my preference is to be with my family. You see, we are similar in a lot of ways, some like to work some like to start a family."

That had Alouette's attention,

"Hi, my name is… yes you know, I feel your answer. Hum, this is different, how do you start a family? Sorry, if that is too personal, I understand."

"The process is much the same as what you would loosely call a 'test tube' newborn. The two of us, yes, female and male add their DNA and four months later, let me introduce my daughter, Sim. And my wife as you would say, Rute."

With that, the humans all were staring at the three together. Sim was smaller in size, but still they couldn't tell the difference between male-female. Without asking, Sparky had their answer,

"You will find the difference in our eyes, females have more slender refined eyes, males a rounder larger eye. It's that simple."

That brought up Perla,

"Hi Sim, very nice to meet you! What do kids your age do to keep busy?"

"Hello Perla, ha-ha do you think I would tell you with my parents right here?"

"Ha-ha your fun! Ok Rute, do you have any other clothes that you wear, say to go to a nice place?"

"Perla, a very nice name, yes we do. Again, we are similar in that regard also. These that we have on, are what you would call work clothes."

Wyatt wanted to jump in,

"This is all so remarkable, I'm trying to think my questions, but for now I'll just talk. Is Element 115 that common or available to everyone?"

Rute "It is. It is mostly found on small moons all around the Galaxy. It is difficult to mine due to the gravity it imposes. Only robotic vehicles that are designed to negotiate the extreme differences are able to process it into useable form.

I am including all present in our conversation even thou I am not speaking, to answer a question you were posing."

Wyatt "Yes thank you. Are there other ways to affect gravity?"

Sim "Yes, the old fashion mercury-fusion centrifuge that you on Earth are starting to experiment with is a start. But it's not a very safe one, or very functional, due to the need of additional 'Jets' to propel the craft."

Richard "Wow, if we ever play some games together, would you be on my team?"

That had all present smiling or amused. It was Sparky next,

"Where are our manors, would you like to have some refreshment or a rest stop?"

Rich "Yes actually, some water possibly?"

"Yes of course, we also have molded likenesses of your Earth restrooms here if you would like. Let me show you over this way, we also have Diet Coke, Pepsi or Hawaiian punch, whatever you like."

That had the Earthlings laughing, Perla and Alouette crowded in with thought and voice,

"Diet Coke, you really can read minds! Yes please!"

Subsequent to the break, the talk settled into a more relaxed feeling and opened a little more along the lines of Science.

Wyatt "Some theories about your race helping us humans along with our DNA have been presented, how much is true?"

Sparky "We have facilitated twice, early on, in approximately ten thousand of your earth years. That was all that was needed. You must understand, yours is not the only planet that needed assistance.

On your Earth, there was a stall in genetics that would have lasted thousands of years to long. We were keeping the neighborhood in balance, not wanting a more advanced race to over run your planet."

Richard "So how many different advanced civilizations are there in our galaxy?"

Sim jumped in with,

"There are thirty-six. One hundred sixty-seven in various stages of metamorphous."

Alouette "When Wyatt and I have children, I want to enroll them in your school!"

Rute "Hum, thank you. Your planet is so very right and desirable, the balance between water and landmass. The large livable zones, and your air."

Wyatt "Are there other civilizations where your help was given?"

"Yes, a few."

Perla "May I ask: Who built the Pyramids?"

"Another race did help with Mathematics and assisted with quarrying limestone and placing. Mostly from a distance, also the central and south American mezzo Pyramids."

Richard "The Inca's stones that have been fitted together so tightly, with a smooth-rounded-edges. I never believed that humans with brass or substandard iron tools could quarry and set large stones like that."

Sparky "Yes, that is correct. Most of those features were accomplished with what you would call, particle beams or lasers. The introduction of the process was heavily debated. Was it too much too soon? The end decision was to leave small areas of demonstration of what to strive for."

Wyatt "Being an Astrophysicist, my next question may sound rude but please understand. Is it an intention of your race or some other to install a new world order?"

Sparky "Our intention is to improve the solar systems balance. That is your planet. You are not headed in a good direction at the moment and need correction. Help will not come from Space. We will never directly impose our will on Earth. Our hope is that you will be able to resolve your own differences soon."

Richard "What about other civilizations that might be more aggressive in trying to handle our differences. Would someone else assume control?"

"Yours is in the third age of Earth. Meaning: either the animal population became disproportional to the environment, or the individuals present were not developing any solid cognitive abilities."

Richard "Who's decision was that?"

Sparky "Chance, mostly."

Wyatt "I understand. Asteroids, meteorites and Exoplanets finding their way to Earth to reshape the past into the future. Happens every day...somewhere."

Sparky "That is correct."

Perla "Here I go with a little Hollywood spin, would a "Annexation" happen?"

"The probability is approximately the same as a XO planet or a massive asteroid striking Earth again. What most people don't understand is that every other being has their own environment that they prosper in. The different percentages of the gasses that make up the air of Earth is common, but not the same as anywhere else. Each civilization is unique along with their planet distance from its Star."

"Oh good, well, I never liked those movies anyway. Speaking, or thinking of that, do you have any similar kind of entertainment for amusement?"

Sim "Yes, we sometimes watch Earth television!"

That had the humans laughing out loud with the others present with small thoughts of joy.

Alouette "Sim, the thought that I just felt was wonderful. For me, it felt like a full feeling of joy, happiness or delight!"

"Yes, that is one reason we prefer to think complete thoughts. This may sound odd, on your Earth, in the Chinese calligraphy, one charter represents a complete thought.

Our communication is much the same. It feels like it holds full meaning."

Alouette "I really will bring our kids here for school!"

That again, gave the earthlings a warm, pleasant impression.

Auch "We must consider a time element for a tour of your Planet. The questions can still continue."

Sparky "Yes, Sim you are excused to study. What we have in mind is a circle of Serpo, and then we will tour one of our city's."

Sim "I would like to attend the tour, and if it's excitable, I would like to sit with Alouette and Perla."

Rute "You do have your father's direct attribute. Then it's up to our guests."

Both the girls answered at once.

"You can sit with me!"

Again, a spacious feeling of cerebral delight passed through the humans.

Chapter 20

The area that they had originally landed in was more or less, a general public meeting location. Noticing the attention they were attracting from the other Serpens, Richard asked,

"Are we somewhat odd?"

Sim "Yes, you look _really_ strange to us!"

With laughs and understanding smiles, they stepped onto a moving sidewalk much like what we have here in our larger Airports. Stopping at what could be easily described as a large domed floating golf cart, they stepped in.

Perla "Ok, let me go first then Sim..."

Al "Then me!"

Sim's parents seemed to be very proud of their little one. The rest were all mixed in rows of comfortable seats.

Sparky "We will start with a polar circumnavigation to give an overview of what landmass we have. Then we will take the equator around to exhibit our oceans."

Richard "Just curious as to the distance and time of one lap?"

Sim "Serpo is 1.9x smaller than Earth so we travel 21,296.9km or 13,233.3mi one way. My Dad will drive slow, so it'll take us about 20 of your Earth minutes."

That had the Earthlings laughing again.

Rute "If you see anything you would like to linger on, go ahead and ask. I'll let Sparky drive- I'll do the talking."

Slowly rising above the structures that weren't very tall, they noted the dome of the car had changed colors. It now appeared as night vision glasses do here on Earth.

All the color was drained away, anything that reflected light or heat was brighter green than the background.

"Would you consider this city one of the largest, or are they starting to all melt together?"

Sim "It's all just about like this. Not very different until we get on a little more. The mountains seam to hold the buildings back."

Wyatt "The speed we are traveling at would melt most metals back on Earth. This car we are in seems to be commonplace, how long does it take us to formulate a likely composite?"

Sparky "You are onto the right ideas and will soon be finding what will be necessary. For a long time, you paid special attention to so-called curates, or compounds containing copper. With these curates, some important progress was made, even though you have many open questions in the theory of **high-temperature superconductivity** today. Your resent work on superconductors will help you along the way, in particular some nickelates additional hydrogen atoms that you have incorporated into your material structures in the experiment.

Some materials are only superconducting near absolute **temperature** zero—such superconductors are not practical for technical applications. Therefore, for decades, you have been looking for materials that remain superconducting even at higher temperatures. Referring too "elevated temperatures" in this context, however, is still very cold: even high-temperature superconductors must be cooled strongly in order to obtain their superconducting properties.

Therefore, your search for new superconductors at even higher temperatures continues.

Our interaction with your government has helped increase the understanding of Element 115 and some other Elements that weren't on your periodic table of elements five years ago.

We are approaching what Sim has been waiting for, our mountains."

Below them, sharp vertical ridges that were a mile high in places, then trailed off into an abyss. Then to rugged plateaus and back up vertically to snow cap tops. Then, seemingly too soon they were back over the same type structures that they started in.

Soon, it was a repeat of the first set of polar mountains.

Sparky "We will be turning here to head out over the sea and to make Sim happy, we will go a bit faster due to the same ness of the sea. There are islands but not very populated. There are very large cities under the water, but that will be for another time."

Arriving back at their start, it was decided that they would spend the night on the larger craft they had arrived on. Auch had made arrangements to dine together, but the Three Serpens would not be present. Their way of energy replenishment or eating, was essentially a bath that was absorbed topically. Obviously, special considerations had to be made for the visitors.

The next morning started with the interior lighting very slowly brightening. With roosters and other morning sounds that were commonly found around the observatory. That started everybody off with a laugh and a smile.

Richard "Auch, you have a sense of humor! Please take no offence, but in all the time I've known you, I never seen this side."

Alouette "I bet it was you that brought the Diet Coke & the other stuff along!"

"It's possible that in my association with you Earthlings an amount of 'fun' has 'rubbed off' on me."

After a light breakfast on board the larger craft, they headed back to meet with Sparky and Rute.

"Hello once again, we do hope your night was comfortable, we would like to take you on a shorter tour of our 'City.' And then, Auch has reminded us that you must return to you Earth."

Alouette "I hope Sim will be with us on our tour?"

Rute "She has School to attend too. She did tell us last night that she enjoyed meeting all of you."

Perla "She was a pleasure to be with. Now I hope we aren't keeping you from something important."

"No, let's see what we have for you."

They were again in the dome G-cart, on this outing they casually fell in with the existing traffic on an imaginary freeway. That raised a few questions from the Earthlings,

Richard "This is amazing! So, the airways can get as wide or as tall as the quantity of traffic increases or decreases?"

Sparky "I have seen your freeways on Earth and know what you are relating to. This would be a good way to deal with that issue. All the resources and labor that is wasted in establishing a fixed driving surface could be better placed. In time, those things will change as long as you don't blow yourselves to pieces."

At that point, all the humans agreed with a small bit of trepidation in their tone. Wyatt had to ask,

"I ask in all sincerity, is there any possibility of help with our human dilemma?"

Auch took up the request,

"We have in the past and will in the future, but only from a shaded point of reference. We will not take sides with any one state. Also, we can't compromise ourselves by landing at any one capital building and presenting ourselves. You as a planet, will need to request our help."

Richard "I have seen a number of launches with questionable payloads be purposely set of course. And I thank you for it. The military branches of most all nations is out of control."

Sparky "Don't be too hard on your Military, most of your troubles come from extremely well financed individuals and small groups. They are quietly in different countries and not limited to just one, they are all around the Earth."

The discussion carried on thus for the rest of the tour, between stopping at various sites common to all City's. They were introduced to what would be considered the Governor, that was very odd.

It was getting to be time for departure, the humans were extremely grateful.

Richard "We have found that we aren't that different in our daily life. I hope that we as ambassadors can make a difference, we will try."

On their thirty-nine-light-year trip back to Earth (in one-hour, Magnetic fields changed) they tried to come up with how to accomplish the end goal of acknowledgement and acceptance.

Some people of planet Earth are not going to get along easily with their newfound neighbors.

Chapter 21

Ambassador Boxer's team that was sent to Wyatt's desert home had again installed bugs and video cameras.

Arriving in the desert at 1:00 AM, the following night Auch had an idea that they had been visited. Settling the craft to hover directly above, he wanted to do a scan of the interior and perimeter.

"As I had assumed, Boxer has reinstalled all different devices, smaller and smarter."

Auch had a pad of his own, and he had a plan,

"I have located 11 devices, all of which I will send a virus that will link your address here and your beach house. That will essentially overheat their main servers critically, damaging all their portable devices in the prosses. In the future, I'll leave one of my own devices here to repeat this prosses if it is attempted again. Do keep records of any physical damage to any of your property at all locations."

Alouette "Auch you have been so very kind I wish we could do something specially for you.

I know you are going to say, but we like what we are trying to do for all concerned. Thank you."

"Well, you are welcome! Then I will see you in eight weeks. Good morning."

Looks like it was back to work for the Earthlings on Monday, but that did give them Sunday, today, to thankfully recuperate around the desert pool.

Chapter 22

Downtown San Diego seemed absolutely beautiful, with the bay and surrounding inclusion's as opposed to the cities of Zeta Reticulin's.

Alouette "I think you're a bit slanted towards your hometown."

Wyatt "What could possibly give you that idea?"

"Oh, just when you say, 'man, I love this town!' out of the blue, That kind of thing."

Enjoying the views of the bay from the Fish Market for a fast lunch, Wyatt & Alouette were having no trouble at all adjusting to Earth. They traded thoughts again on how to introduce their off-planet neighbors to us slow minded Earthlings.

Wyatt "Maybe we could have a worldwide guessing game. Guess how many different civilizations have visited Earth. Or maybe something else, but the grand prize would be a trip for two, Destination: Saturn! Spent the weekend floating amongst the rings and touring the moons of Jupiter!"

Al "Your nuts."

"Well, that sure would get the world's attention! You know, I better ask Auch if that would be ok…"

"Let's be a little more 'down to Earth' and order lunch so we can get back to work at a reasonable time!"

Their company was downtown, and offices in the same building, his side and her side. Nevertheless, they found themselves together whenever they could. Still thinking of ways to 'enlighten' their human counterparts without derision.

The standing issue was 'Star people.' How would they even say that aloud without the Government's large footprint on their throat.

Auch had already told them that they would not intercede in any major human conflict in a public way.

Times and troubles tarry on, arriving back at their respective offices, an individual was waiting,

"Hello are you Wyatt Cantu?"

"Yes, and who might you be?"

Handing an envelope to Wyatt, turning and leaving without a word.

Before he could call her, his phone rang.

"Hay, I just got a summons! Can you believe it!"

"Welcome to the club, I know who the ass wipe is that started it too!"

Al "I'm gonna call Auch..."

Wyatt "Well, how about maybe let this run for a little while. I'd like to see where this might be going."

Al "You think? Alright, I'll settle a little, but not for long!"

Wyatt then called their Attorney, to enquire of the case and to be present on the appearance date.

Meeting in court, the bailiff read off the charges, but the main charge was,

"Willful destruction of all mainframe and portable communication devices."

The Judge had to be reminded that the plaintiff had illegally vandalized and forced their way into two private residences and destroyed a pair of entry doors on a public observatory.

The Judge seemed not to care and wanted to know what Wyatt and Alouette were concealing that made the plaintiff focus on the two in the first place.

In a quick conference, it was decided that this was the place to bring up the elephant in the room, Extra Terrestrial Beings. The attorney brought up,

"My clients were given very valuable technology that they were exclusively entrusted with. It will be our action now, to bring a counter suit of; intentional premediated theft, and willful destruction of privet and public property. Thank you for the Courts time."

Of course, there was abundance of boiling and popping from the plaintiffs. All Court proceedings would resume when the appropriate added charges were filed.

In the meantime, back at the beach, the two Earthlings were getting in touch with Auch to update him on the latest.

"It seemed to be an effective way to slowly introduce the idea of off worlders. Our idea is to get a jury and mid-way into presenting the evidence, we introduce the ETB side. What do you think?"

Auch "I am unwilling to make a public appearance or reveal any of the functions on the Moon. But will help in any other way possible."

Wyatt "That will do just fine."

Auch "Is it your wish for me to remove my virus introduction device from your home?"

Al "No, I say keep it there! I don't want his people in my home ever! If they do it again, it will just prove that they are malicious awful people!"

102

Wyatt "That will be our answer if they do try it again."

Another court date for pre-trial in two weeks was set. Time had already run away from them, and soon after that date, they would be leaving for the Moon.

Alouette "My thought is we land on the courthouse steps, exit the craft and go ask the jury if they would like a ride?! That would be nice and direct."

Wyatt "Ha-ha, you crack me up, but I have a better one, skip the jury, I'm going straight for the Judge! I am serious. Well, not about landing on the courthouse, but I could ask Auch to bring the small ETV and maybe land in his back yard.

My point is, maybe we could give him or her, don't know who our permanent Judge is yet, a ride to the Moon."

Al "Yeah, maybe, but Auch may not go for that. How about the Governor, or some political figure?"

Wyatt "Think, a little more down home…"

Chapter 23

All the Discovery portions on both sides had started and Court dates had been set to begin in two months. At present, the four ambassadors were enjoying a layered desert sun set.

Perla "It's so nice to be here again, thank you. Oh, and thanks for the preferred settee seating."

Alouette "That is the least we could offer to the best girl in the world!"

Perla for fun added,

"Yes, don't forget Hot!"

That was for a long time going to be their group standing joke, and had its intended effect, smiles and laughs.

Richard "What do you think Boxer is going to come up with this time, are we going to come back home only to find our tires have been slashed?!"

Wyatt "I have something that's going to take the focus off us, and really zero in on Boxer."

Al "What aren't you telling me?"

Wyatt "That Richard isn't the only one who can keep secrets!"

Midnight was the intended departure time, aboard the craft, Auch had seated everyone but Wyatt. He was waiting out on the dark road for his guest to arrive. He was getting concerned although, it had already been twenty minutes and he couldn't keep Auch waiting.

Calling Al, "Hi, I'll give him five more minutes then we will go... wait, I see headlights..."

Chapter 24

Entering the United Galaxy hall with hopeful anticipation, the ambassadors took their seats. The last one to seat himself was situated next to Boxer. It did have its intended affect.

"You are... you can't be... how did you get... you can't be here!!"

With a very calm demeaner he was very use too, their guest introduced himself,

"Sure as saints be, I be here. And from what be known bout your confessions, I mita become a permanent reminder!"

An all most blubbering Ambassador Boxer found his words,

"Fa-Father O'Neill! It's a great honor to have you here!"

The man of the cloth gave his patron a twisted sour look. He was very familiar with Boxer and his family and knew they were steadfastly devout Catholic. Boxer's wife ran their house with more than just words, she also was known to wield a weighty frypan!

Farther O' "So, you can't have urn way at home, ya come up here en run yur tongue! I duny kin where ta start with your penance!"

The interchange had drawn some attention from the surrounding ambassadors.

Some were adjusting their earpieces on their translators too better understand what the interchange held. The entire time, the four Earthlings had large smiles and were holding back laughter. It was now time to come to order, so all were requested to take their seats.

The Speaker of the house welcomed all the ambassador's present, and those on all the displays around the general assembly hall.

"First I would direct my remarks to the Ambassador Boxer from Earth. Due to this, the second admonishment for indiscretion directed at fellow Ambassador's, Mr. Boxer will be expelled on one further infraction. This is your last warning."

The audience was rightly silent. Boxer didn't have a verbal response due to his overwhelming disbelief and rancor of the Speaker. He had taken the first warning as just lip service for the infractions against the new Ambassador's two sessions ago. He honestly couldn't put any real words together but responded with,

"Noted"

The real fun started in that night outside the meeting hall,

Farther O' "So's ya know, it's not just me that's see'n the devil at work in ye. It's even the good peoples of the Moon! Christ Almighty! Father forgive me for standing in the presents of the devil himself!"

The other Earthlings were wanting to be elsewhere,

Richard "Father O'Neill, we are headed for dinner and would like to invite any that would like to come along..."

Father O' "You see Boxer, that is the kindness of God himself! Including one's enemies at the table!

Richard my boy, I thanks ye, but this one will be needing my attention privately."

So, with contented smiles the four walked with easy steps to their favored dinner under a dome setting.

The view was something that obviously mesmerized all of them. Al, Wyatt and Perla still were having trouble getting use to the floating 'coffee can' servers.

"Well, that was really a show today Assembly men and women. May I take your drink orders?"

Wyatt "You heard about all that up here?"

"Oh yes, we like to take an active part in our community."

That confounded all the humans farther.

Perla "I'm sorry I haven't asked sooner, what would you like to be referred too?"

"We are called Zonies. Like you humans, we have names we pick for ourselves. My name is Tart. Thank-you for asking. Would you each like the same thing you usually order?"

Alouette "Tart, that's very nice, yes at least for me..."

At that moment they were interrupted by another floating Zonie.

"May I deliver a message? (Yes) This is From Ambassador Boxer."

Handing an envelope to Richard, then departing.

"Yes Tart, we will all have the same thing, Thanks."

Perla "A formal apology?"

Wyatt "I really don't think so, he's too one sided."

Rich "Well let's see...Blab-bla, if you think your stunt has any bearing on my efforts to keep my country safe you are mistaken. On an on..."

Alouette "I think we are dealing with a few mental issues here under one roof. Would it be safe to say, we should just let this alone, or ignore that person altogether?"

Wyatt "No, this is just a very cheap ploy to redirect us. I think we need to focus on all the contacts that he is furthering along up here. What I mean is, follow the money trail.

Why is he being so defensive? I think he's trying to find out that same stuff about us. Only difference is, we don't have any money to leave a trail with. Unless he thinks we are big players funded by another country."

Richard "Ha-yeah that's us."

That did lighten the feelings, along with the drinks that Tart just delivered.

Al "But how deep? You know he's in all the way up to his neck. All his military background stuff is got to be covered-up so much we will never get at it. Personally, I've got no idea how to follow any of that stuff, we have tried being nice, let's try something else."

Wyatt "I know you don't like uninvited people in our homes, and I completely agree. We have been nice too long."

Richard "Cool, I have a 45 and a few 9mm's, oh and a 12 and 20 gauge, Perla likes to shoot skeet".

Wyatt "Woo- let's not meet at high noon just yet. I'm just suggesting not acknowledging so much him here. We have too back on earth in the lawsuit, that's our argument we're using to make the general public aware of our ET cousins."

Perla "Doesn't he have friends? If he is as wacked out as he seems, is it possible to have normal friend's, maybe find out about them?"

Alouette "That sounds sorta terrible, but I'm thinking that if we had children, he would leverage them in some way possibly. And I really don't go for 'an eye for an eye' kinda thinking, but we are dealing with the personal attracts on us and future of the Earth!"

108

The talk continued on into the night.

Chapter 25

At the end of the week on the short trip back to Earth, had them quickly asking Father O'Neill what progress if any, was made.

"He a lost sheep, convinced his way is the soundest. I must thank you for this time being closer to God. I must also give you my greatest thank you for introducing me to God's other children, completely amazing! As for what we agreed on, I'll hold my tongue until you give me permission to speak."

All were very grateful to Father O'Neill for the attempt and hope something good would come of it.

Back among the work-a-day world, new evidence had surfaced that had linked the four to supposed interests in Eastern Europe. It was amazing what people will invent to further their causes. The four weren't too concerned having never been to or had any paper dealings with any overseas financial institutions.

Like so much trash that is in the places of power today, people lie and add untruth to all of their public statements. Too large a measure of the general population, like so many people, excepting what they hear without question, just because that one individual said it.

The attorneys had easily put together, four very precise timelines countering the bogus claims against the four defendants.

These are the times through discovery that can be most turbulent. How much information to expose now or wait and hold for later and were putting together a story board of their own. That all was for the attorneys and the people that they had hired,

Alouette or Wyatt had no experience with the Law, and they were very glad about that. It was all such an abysmal witness for humanity, that every difference had to be brought up in a court of law. What was worse, there are some people that enjoy it.

He decided to change things up, calling his secretary and asking for a group of reservations and plane tickets, he surprise her with a call,

"You know what I think?"

Al "Mostly things like what's the mass of a moon orbiting a planet a hundred light years away, things of that nature..."

"You know you sound so pretty when you make things up on the fly..."

"Oh, come on, thanks, you can't even see me... Let's go home, I'm tired of my office."

"How about we stop off for dinner over on Newport Ave. first. I have something for you."

"Ok, I think I know the little Mexican place that you have in mind. See you there."

South of the border surrounding's and drinks in hand,

"How was your day?"

Alouette "I had a good one. I must say, I agree with whoever said our earth jobs are going to get boring."

"I'll take credit for that! And I agree with you, so you and I are going to the Cayman Islands for ten days. We leave on Sunday."

There was a different mixture of unexpected surprised that lit-up Alouette's pretty face. Most of all, it was a feeling that she conveyed that said, 'that's exactly what I need.' He loved giving and receiving her smiles this moment.

Al "I wonder if it was a couple of the travel/diving magazines I have left around the house that gave you the idea…"

"All those were for the deep south pacific, Sri Lanka, or Seychelles. It would take us three days on an airplane. Hay, maybe we could ask Auch to drop us off somewhere."

Al "No, let's just fly commercial. We need a reminder of what it's like to travel like the rest of humanity. I wonder if our passports are still valid."

"All done. So, we have all day to pack tomorrow, Houston first, then off to the Caribbean!"

The issue of flying together was always a touchy one, they both loved to fly. So, the choice of the window seat always had to be up to chance.

Wyatt "Heads or Tails…"

Calling it in the air,

"Tails…Ha-ha!"

She lightly clapping her hands and jumping little jumps.

"Yeah, it's about time, you got it the last two trips. Besides, you booked first class, so you won't have the middle seat. Come on now, let me see a little smile…"

"Sounds like your practicing for parenthood, I guess I'll get use to putting little people first."

Alouette "Oh brother, such a difficult lot you are given."

112

(Almost to Huston)

"Why is taking so long? Are we there yet? Hay how bout flipping for the window seat on the next leg?"

Al "No, I tried that one before and you told me that the coin toss was good all day long. My goodness, going to the Moon in three minutes, thirty-nine light years in an hour and a half! We are on my same page, because I was thinking the very thing!"

"Four hours on an airplane is a long time, especially way over here away from the window."

"I know, hum, we're almost there. I think I'll throw everything in the room then head for the beach. First, I'll get a tropical punch of some kind, then float in the water!"

"That's really nice of you to get all our stuff up to the room while I go straight to the water, tell you what; I'll pick up a drink for you."

Al "Listen here buster..."

Landing in Grand Cayman and finding their way to the luggage, then hotel transfer, Alouette saw something that made her stop.

Wyatt "Did you forget something?"

"No, I guess it's nothing. Let's go get in the water!"

Settling into their beach front Resort, standing chest high in 88° tranquil water with their drink of choice,

"I'm going to make sure I keep sunscreen polished all over you. Your beautiful black hair is in mindful contrast to your light coloring."

"I just spray it all over really quick."

"Hum, I think I'll reintroduce you to the old fashion way of application by hand. It's a sure way to keep your area's..."

They nudged themselves in and out of the water for refills twice more while the sunset put on a tropical pageant.

Spending a slow time getting ready for dinner that evening, for a semi-formal English Caribbean arrangement, Wyatt commented as he was seating Alouette,

"First, I would like to tell you that just a little sun gives you an even more devastating appearance than you naturally give off."

That did give her pause, she softly took his hand,

"The Caribbean sun seems to have done the same to your handsome presence. And thank you."

Lost with themselves in a room of thirty others for a brief time, adjusting back,

"So tomorrow we get to go on a drift dive, do you remember which way your regulator attaches to the nitrox tank?"

Al "You know I always get it right the first time, ha-ha."

"Well, me too. We've never done one of these, I'm kinda jazzed about it."

"Me too! I hope the water is a clear as the travel magazines say."

"I hope so, hay, I wanted to ask you about what you were thinking when we left the airport today, before I forget."

"Your just gonna think I'm seeing things, but I thought I saw Boxer."

"Really, this would be the last place I would think a tight nut like that would bother with. I can't picture him in shorts."

"Well I don't want too, and he wasn't. He had on a three-piece suit and carrying a briefcase. I notice him over by all the limos that were waiting for people."

"That's really odd don't you think, now I'm thinking we should have followed the guy."

"Oh I don't think so, no! I'm so glad we did just what we did! Let's do the same thing tomorrow night!"

Exchanging feelings and knowing looks and touches only lovers do.

Chapter 26

The following day was fantastic! The water clarity was like none other! Slowly drifting with the current for 40 minutes was fantastic! Like flying 10-20ft. above the reef with small kicks of the fins to adjust the distance off the reef. They made plans for another dive in two days, but for now they were getting ready for a cruise around town.

Al "Ok, I have to get the hottest girl in the world something, so that means shopping!"

Wyatt "Oh joy."

"Come on, you like it, you're just saying that to protect your masculinity. It's a secret that is safe with me."

"Yeah, how about we stop for lunch at 2:00. That will give me some reflection time."

"It's 1:30 now and we aren't even off the shuttle!"

"Aren't you starved? I am, it was a long float, remember we didn't have breakfast."

"Ok, you want ta just start there?"

"There you go, once again, perfect idea's…"

Finding a very nice restaurant overlooking the water, studying their menus,

"Oh me gee…"

"What is so outstanding!"

"It is him! Don't look!"

All this was in a very quiet voice.

"Boxer is here, and I don't think that's his daughter!"

"If that is true, he's found a very out of the way place for that kind of thing. I've been thinking, he's putting money away here and avoiding taxes. Are they just ordering or are they done?"

"Looks like their almost done."

"Then just get something for yourself. I want to follow them. If you can kinda keep hidden I don't want to give ourselves away."

"They are way over there on the other side."

"How did you spot him?"

"Easily, his horsehair toupee.'"

That gave them some other things to laugh at, Al had a salad and Wyatt picked at it a little. It wasn't long before Boxer left.

"I'll call you as soon as I find something out."

This was all new for Wyatt, he'd seen this routine in all the films, but it felt out of place right now. It seemed easy enough, grab a cab, easily did the same. But it was all different, the traffic was light, even so, it was looking like he lost him. He was explaining to the driver,

"Shoot, lost him! I can't see him, anymore can you?"

"You want to go where Eimear is going?"

"Aum, who's Eimear."

"That cab we was following; you want to go where he went?"

"Yes, that would be great."

"All us guys know each other, let me call him."

He did just that.

"Ok, he is taking the girl to a casino, then man is going to a big bank."

"I see, well I guess just take me back where we started…"

Giving Al a call, and easily catching up with her at a tourist's trap.

"What did you find?"

"I think he really is dumping money down here. I have no idea what for, you go ahead for a while, I'm calling the attorneys."

With all the new business out of the way for now, they spent the rest of the day working on good old business, the sunset found them back in the water chest deep.

"I think this is going to be a requirement that we attend to each night about this time."

"I Like it!"

Chapter 27

Not so easily getting back into the San Diego routine, they did comfort themselves with the thought of their "other Moon job."

Alouette "People around my office are asking if they can get a vacation schedule like mine. I remind them that our last name is on the letter head. Sounds mean, but that's just the truth."

"Sorta like that over on my side, except it's only the distant stars that request more attention. Sounds kinda uppity, who would even bring that up with you?"

"Oh you know…the best girl in the world, you know that one…"

Laughing, and finish putting things in the car for Borrego, they would be leaving for the Moon in two days from the desert. On the drive over, they were trying to put together a requisition for help from the other delegates. Boxer not included. It would be a request for suggestions on how to inform the human race that there are other neighbors out amongst the solar system.

Wyatt "You know, the big looming reason all the Government people are using to avoid telling people: Catastrophic social breakdown due to religious beliefs."

Alou "Oh yeah, but I have a feeling that most people have seen so much of the 'Man from Mars' on TV that they just expect to meet one sooner or later."

"You think? The way a large swath of people are blindly following along the latest ass wipe in the white house, I wonder…"

"Hay, you know I don't like swearing but regarding that, I don't think I mind much. I'm gonna ask Auch about his views on religion, seems odd one of us haven't asked about that already."

"Yeah kinda."

Settling in for the sunset, (Richard stopped for their favorite Mex to go place before getting to Wyatt's place) passing around different orders and plastic forks.

Wyatt "Has the question of religion come up without me noticing it? I mean, have you two talked with Auch about that?"

Rich "I think all the science and new horizons have taken over, at least for me. So no, I haven't brought that up with him."

Perla "You know your right; we didn't ask about any of that when we were with Sparky either. We really should have asked Sim; I think she would have given us all the straight facts."

That brightened the small group.

Meeting Auch again in the quiet of the desert after midnight, they found themselves enjoying the shimmering sparkles of the 'plasma' waterfall entering the hanger on the Moon before the question came back to mind.

Richard "Hay Auch, question for you, do you believe in God?"

"We were wondering when that question was going to be asked. Yes."

Alouette "I knew it!"

"Since our time began over millions of you earth years ago, we knew there was a positive guiding force. One not to be trifled with."

Wyatt "That will be a very encouraging factor in our telling of life in our Galaxy to our Earth-bound humans."

Auch "Since I have you all here, let me bring you up to date on our thoughts. I know we have had issues with Boxer, but we have felt that parts of his plan to populate the moon with humans could be a good thing."

Perla "Well, there are five humans here now and already it's four against one! But I understand the attraction of having earthlings here, I know there would be friendly contact here. And the idea of the introduction here on the moon, would be more of a neutral ground at least to the humans."

Auch "That is exactly our hope. Our introduction en way of 'landing on the White House lawn' would carry a threatening invasion appearance. Here, things would present themselves in a 'welcome to the club' manor, we think."

Rich "So, you are asking us to be nice to this guy and find out how far he wants to take things."

Auch "Yes."

Wyatt "We can and will, won't we Alou..."

"Well, for the enlightenment of the human race, ok. After that a restraining order goes into place back on Earth!"

Perla "I totally get it. I don't like uninvited anything either!"

Richard "We will handle it just fine. Now we are here and have a job to do... let's go."

Stopping for some breakfast at the creator view food court, each one was thoughtfully quiet for a time,

Richard breaking the silence,

"I know it pains us all, especially Alouette and Wyatt, but we gotta sound interested in what Boxer has in mind. I'll be the representative for us, so the rest of you can relax an not worry about being nice if that's ok with you."

Everybody easily agreed and left that issue alone.

Chapter 28

Getting past the first day's activities, all the Ambassadors were preparing to depart, Richard let his group know he would meet them at dinner. Stepping over to Boxer,

"Ambassador, I have a question: What are some of the programs that you have introduced prior to our installation here. I have only heard from others about an idea to place humans here for a long term."

Boxer "So now you want to glam-on too my programs now do you?"

"I understand we have started off a little bumpy, but here we are, and I want to get caught up. I assure you; we have no intention to interrupt or change any ideas you are involved with."

A longer meeting was scheduled, for now proposal documents were exchanged. After a brief look at some of the projects, Richard found that everything Boxer was encouraging had a very heavy military flavor. Trying to ask questions that didn't provoke his host, which carried a difficulty factor of 7 out of 10,

"I see the portion of the plans for commercial business-like mining or a type of manufacturing are quite small. Wouldn't that be one of the biggest reasons to be here in the first place, trade with other civilization's?"

Almost looking over his shoulder, checking side to side,

"We must be ready to defend ourselves!"

Stated in a whisper with a clenched jaw,

Richard "Against who?"

Boxer with a wide sweep of his arm,

"THEM!"

Richard had to check himself emotionally from outwardly expressing disbelieve and wonder at the sanity of the person standing opposite him. Instead, he appeared to assume the role of an enthusiastic new recruit with all the trappings. Quickly looking around and lowering his voice,

"All of them?"

Boxer knowingly reassured him,

"Almost all. They are trying to befriend us now, that's why they keep asking us about our resources. Don't give them any detailed information on anything. If they do ask for details, change the numbers to reflect a lower amount of output."

"Alright, thanks for letting us know. I should have talked with you sooner. Any one race that seems to be especially abrasive?"

"Those little gray ones. They are always asking me about our military and how much of a presence we intend to place here."

"Well then, what are your plans regarding that."

Boxer "98% will be active military."

Richard, up until this point, was still acting like the excitable young recruit, but now,

"That much, seems a bit excessive, speaking of that, I haven't noticed any military anything here in the small city."

"It is all hidden on another part of the Moon."

Rich "Well then, I'll ask Auch to show us that location, he's been very accommodating."

"He won't admit to anything, I'm sure of it. Everyone here has been so nice to us, as far as I am concerned that translates into cover-up."

Richard, taking into consideration the past tactics of Boxer, now understood he was dealing with an unbelievable left over from WW2 era. He wanted control of whatever he could get his hands on. Right now, he needed to talk with Auch, so deciding to kindly retreat, he invited him to dinner with the others, knowing he wouldn't include himself.

"No, that's not possible, since I am in a lawsuit with the other two on Earth. We will continue our talks at another time."

Thankfully alone on his way up to the dome, he thought to stop for a moment and leave a message on Auch's pad. Auch responded with,

"May I invite myself to dinner?"

"Of course, I'm at the elevator now and will have a place setting added."

Following a lot of requests for information, Richard asked,

"Let me wait until Auch gets here, then we can get into it. For now, Tart may I request an additional place setting and of course my usual beverage?"

And before you could say, I'll have another, she was back with the request. Auch was soon to join the table, and the information gained was shared.

Richard "These are his words and don't reflect our views here. His plans are for a small city, with 98% of it a military installation. He is convinced that almost all of the aliens are trying to overrun the Earth. He also told me that there are secret alien military bases here on the Moon. I'm not inflating or changing anything that was said."

Even Auch was a little taken back, the others were a little surprised, but not overly so.

Auch "I can state categorically that there is no 'military' anywhere on this moon or lingering in space which is something that I cannot say about your government presently."

Wyatt "Is what you are referring to 'Star Wars' Regan era satellite installations, we know about that."

Auch "They are maned installations in case you didn't know."

A collective "What?!"

The evening carried on back at their suite with more thoughts on how to approach the problem.

Auch "I wonder if your Father O'Neal could use the 'fear of God' as a consequence of excessive military buildup."

Richard "I have a good feeling that he is too far gone. For something like this, I believe he would say one thing then do another even to Father O'Neal. Could we possibly encourage the project to get it out in the open, and then have the United Council turn it down?"

It continued on for a time, but nothing was decided. The next day was met with a surprise, Boxer extended a request for Richard too ride along with him on a small tour.

"Your two friends can hold our place; I wish to show you what I was discussing too yesterday. My assistant will drive us out to the sights I was referring too and a review of my chose of locations for our improvements."

Richard was a little taken back but excepted gratefully.

Heading towards the hanger, Boxer was giving Richard some size particulars on the above grade establishments and guesses on the size of the underground complex. Richard had to question Boxer regarding his assistant's piloting abilities,

"Is your lieutenant a telepathic, can he fly?"

"No, of course not, I don't want to waste time with that nonsense.

They have vehicles that we humans can fly, and they seem not to be bothered with where we go. Shall we."

The craft looked like a floating SUV with a clear dome. The controls looked just like an earthbound SUV, steering wheel, accelerator and brake pedal.

"Well yes that does look familiar. How far out is the complex?"

"It's about 15 minutes too the first one, and 10 to the second one. Then on around to our new sight on the facing side of the moon."

On the way, Richard was questioning what would be the end goal with his program.

"Human control of the Moon nothing less of course. Since most of what is going on here is almost all robotic anyway, it would mean a simple displacement of some of the aliens."

Richard realized he was going to spend most of the morning with this mentally challenged person, so he didn't want to get combative. Thinking instead of how he would deal with people on earth that were like minded.

"We would need a lot of people here to accomplish that goal, where would the money come from to do that?"

"That's not my area of concern, my military counterparts worry about that. We need to keep our planet safe for humans and only humans."

Arriving at the first location, they hung off to observe from a small distance. It was a large dome that was visibly used for growing food stuffs, but Boxer had a different theory.

"You see a farm but it's not, it's what's under all that. Vast tunnels that house manufacturing of weapons and training facility. And there is another one with the same function."

Richard carefully asked,

"You have had a chance to see the facility firsthand?"

His lieutenant answered,

"I have reconnoitered this installation; it is on an unchecked large scale."

Very matter of fact and very military sounding. Richard at this point was convinced these people were very dangerous.

Moving through the other two sights, then back to Lono City for lunch break with his own group.

"I'm planning on seeing Auch for the rest of the day, so I'll see you at dinner. This guy is honestly nuts. I'll tell you all about it tonight, anything happen that was notable in the morning session?"

Perla casually smiling,

"They found dinosaur bones here on the moon and don't want to tell anyone on Earth!"

Richard didn't even stop chewing,

"Yeah, we passed by that dig, the big monolith was still standing from that old movie 2001, I noticed it was still in that same pit".

Everybody had a good laugh,

Richard "It's really nice to be back with normal regular people!"

Chapter 29

"As you can see, all we have here is hydroponic and dirt farming, they grow what you had for lunch today."

Auch had immediately put Richard in a transport, drove him out to the first sight and introduced him to the staff at the first and second stops that he had visited from a far.

Richard had told Auch that it wasn't necessary but Auch wanted him to take pictures of all the underlying areas.

"This is for you to use when push comes to shove. I understand that you trust me, but you may need something to exhibit too others in the future."

Touring the immense facilities was very impressive, all the robotics were fascinating, all the timing of each one so close in the field, then off 500 yds away, then back and forth. Richard had more questions,

"Where is all the o2 coming from?"

"Well, we make bulk oxygen in a laboratory at each sight. Hydrogen peroxide is poured into many large conical tanks containing some manganese IV oxide. The gas produced is collected in an upside-down gas tank filled with water, just like you would on Earth."

Richard "So that's where the different readings are coming from, it's leaching up through the ground. How many of these farms are there here on the Moon?"

"There are 10 in total. Each one has different food elements growing for some devitrification. If you would like we can visit all the locations, but we will need more time to do that."

"Auch, you're the best, and I don't need to do that.

Something just came to mind, what planet manufactures the different craft for our transportation?"

"You, I'm sure noticed all the different types and kinds in the hanger bays. Each Civilization has their own take on what works best for the body type of that planet. So, to get to your question it takes a planet with more size and diversity than what we have here."

"Ok, but could you if you brought in all the correct resources?"

"I'll say no, because the crafts themselves are almost conscious. Each craft is virtually 'grown,' is the closest word I can think of."

"Wow! I'll ask about all that later, let's get back, I've taken to much of your time... wait, I do have one more request. My I show you the location of Boxers proposed human encampment experiment?"

Auch "Of course, let's be on the way."

Traveling the same loop that he had that morning; Richard was worried about something.

"Ok, here we are, is there any special significance about this particular location. I mean any subterranean geological reason that this place is superior to anywhere else?"

"This is close enough to our north pole and behind a very large impact crater. If military use is intended, this would be a very desirable location. They would have cover from any direct line of attack from Earth, they would position their defenses on the outside of the high creator wall. The main compound behind wouldn't receive any direct attack intensity."

"Is this close to any of your developed areas?"

"No, nothing up here. Farther north there is some water reclamation plants, but that is all."

They had enough touring, so they headed back to Lono city. Meeting up with the other three humans at dinner, Richard reviewed the days findings.

"There is a very serious mental break that's taken over our two colleagues from Earth, and I'm being kind. They literally sit outside of something and make things up. Even when Boxer sends his lieutenant in to inspect an installation, he contrives realities that only bolster the military buildup."

Wyatt "Hay, do you know if we use gravity enhancement in any of our general public corporations other than the military?"

Richard "I have no idea about that. Have to ask Auch, what are you thinking about?"

"I was thinking, if you could get one of those tunneling machines, you've seen the giant nuclear-powered ones that melt rock and then apply it to the inside of the tunnel as they move along. If they could lift that off Earth, and just use regular rockets to push it around in space, they could make a lot of headway fast!"

Al "After what we've seen, I'm sure it's possible but would Auch know about stuff like that?"

Perla "I'm gonna ask him next time I see him; I think I know where you're going with this idea and it's scary. Especially with who is in the White House at the moment."

Al "Couldn't agree with you more. We still need to get a hold of some kind of blueprint, something we can refer to and show a sane group of people."

Richard "Yeah, great! That means I have ta keep my smiley face plastered on around that guy. Excuse me but crap!"

The following morning, back in the council chambers, Richard had the unfortunate task of finding a neutral starting point.

"Mr. Boxer are you individually aware of the interior functions of the two sights we visited. What I am getting at is; the o2 increase in the atmosphere is due to all the farming at those and eight other sights".

"You mean to tell me there are ten of those places! How did you find them out?"

Boxer's haughty expression exposed a long personal episode of excessive insult to all humanity, a slap in the face, another issue of alien imperialism.

At that moment, Richard had to reconstruct a personal profile of the ambassador that was previously low to begin with. How could a person function in this world given the reality he was living in. Loosely propped up truths with no foundation for any lasting integrity to build on. He didn't want to be insulting, but he couldn't help himself...

"I asked my host."

"Well of course! That's a distraction from the two sights we visited. Don't worry we can see through that smoke screen; we will let them think they have us fooled."

At this junction, Richard just let it go,

"Yeah, I guess so. Hay, how big is the 'base' going to be? Do you have any physical plans?"

At that, the meeting was called to order.

Chapter 30

Finishing the week with a feeling like driving on a bent rim, knowing the rest of the car won't take it much longer without shaking apart, Richard seemed happy on the ride home to Earth.

"Hay Wyatt, I'm so pleased that you have to deal with that Boxer guy for eight weeks and I don't!"

"Ha ha, we are doing it for the advancement of the human rase, thankfully the Lawyers are the ones that get most of the face time.

Auch again paused in an invisible hover over the desert home, scanning the interior,

"It appears they again have left a smaller amount of listing devices. Would you like the system cleared?"

Alouette "Yes PLEASE! Can you increase the virus amplitude to include any surrounding connected phones, laptops and computers?"

Auch "I understand your privacy has been violated for the third time. Wyatt, is this also a wish of yours?"

"Absolutely."

"This will undoubtably be added to the proceedings on the legal field."

Al "Looking forward to it."

Turning back to the controls with a slight smile on his face he initiated the command.

Wyatt "I think this is going to change the arraignment on the Moon!"

132

Perla "Hay Al, has that guy ever called you two on your regular phones?"

"No, I don't think so."

As the door slid quietly open the warm desert air flooded in, thanking Auch for everything, Alouette had an idea,

"It's hot out tonight! Would you like to come in for something cool to drink? You can leave your craft on 'invisible' for a while, can't you?"

Thinking for a moment,

"Yes, that would be nice."

The humans were very honestly flattered, so Al & Perla went out of their way to make him comfortable.

Al "It will take a few minutes for the air conditioning to come on and get that melted plastic smell out, would you like some ice cream or something to drink?"

"I will have ice cream thank you."

That started a search between the freezer in the garage and the house fridge. Perla bring all the assorted flavors from the garage, along with what Al fond she started reading off the list,

"Rocky Road, and my favorite, Pralines & Cream, Peach Candy and we have sherbets in two flavors!"

Without a que, Perla was getting all the necessary items out and ready to serve up.

"I believe it's proper to follow the hostess's likes, so, Pralines & Cream thank you."

After a few minutes each one contently clinking away with their spoon's & ice cream bowls, enjoying the very comfortable company and surroundings.   A time to turn to Auch's personal side,

Alouette "Where is your family, I apologize for taking so long to ask, we all have been a bit overwhelmed with all that's taken place."

"They are doing well, my home planet is in the Alnitak system, Zeta Orionis in Orion's Belt, first on the left. There are several different civilizations close by, that we trade with.

But back to the family, I have two sons and two daughters. As you would say, my wife, is doing well and is close by, I plan to bring her to the Moon for a time. I feel a need to introduce you each too her."

Alouette "Well you certainly better!"

Perla "What are the kids up too?"

"All either in school or involved with interplanetary business. They have seen my involvement in public service as too much time away from home."

Wyatt "I'll remember that when we have kids..."

Alou "Me too. How long is that burnt silicon smell going to last, not that I really care. I actually like the smell of a setback!"

"We must be cautious; this latest event has a broader circle of devices affected. No doubt be on your guard, they will defiantly retaliate."

A small time passed, Auch kindly thanked them all and bid them adieu,

"I will see you in eight weeks, each of you keep in mind to be cautious now of what you say and where you are. Call me any time for assistance. Thank you for the ice cream, I am going to request a flavor addition to the menu on the Moon."

Each one smiled with thankfully amazed understanding and sent him off to the Moon.

Chapter 31

"WHAT! EVERYTHING!"

A very on top of things office manager with a depth of understanding well beyond the person she worked for, delivered the new message with a savvy that Boxer did not like.

"Apparently, due to some words spoken recently to someone somewhere, the only things working here are the personal cellphones. All the hard drives are toast, and the building mainframe is a hot pile of crap. There is a message for you from your 'long distance associates,' I think that you should listen to it. It's very important."

Boxer "Out with it, what do they want!"

"Well, they don't want you around."

"What are you talking about!"

"According to the message, your services are no longer needed. Your statice as an Ambassador is terminated. Mail will deliver your personal items. The transport services are no longer available to you. This last infraction counts as the third and last tolerated offence. No other recourse is possible."

"This is all an inside plot! It is those new people they are the ones that should be removed! Call our attorneys get them going on to all this!"

"You call 'em, I quit."

As she hung up the phone, she had a thought, maybe why not call the new people. With another fast though, she anticipated their first feelings... why in the world would they trust me? Well, she just fired herself so why not at least try.

Copying their numbers and info, she started putting all her personal things in a book box.

Finding an inner light-sprite helping her justify this abrupt decision to leave a place she didn't like anyway.

Others in the small office had overheard what happened and she noticed one other doing the same.

"Hay Carter, this doesn't have anything to do with the rest of you, it's only my decision to leave."

"I know Sophie, I think it's time for my boot heals to be wandering…"

"Ha-ha well ok Bob!"

"Figured you for 60's protest music. Na, I'm a service guy that doesn't like the way Boxer see's things."

They both went about clearing their desk's out, and of course, some others came over to wish her well. Carter was being as casual as he could, and was trying to time his exit with hers, over his shoulder he asked,

"Need a hand with anything?"

"No… but wait, I think I have left about five or so jackets/overcoats here, if you don't mind. Looks like your box is pretty light, if you wouldn't mind taking the boxes and I'll grab my things out of the closet, and I'll meet you in the parking structure."

He had waited for a chance like this for a time to be away from the office to get to know her a little better, among other things. He knew what car she drove since they all arrived at the same time every morning. Seeing her arms full and keys dangling in hand, he quickly met her at the elevator and,

"Keys please, trunk or back seat?"

Speaking over the large arm load,

"Thanks, passenger side thanks."

"Your box goes in the trunk?"

"That would be great."

All things in their place,

"It looks like our free spirits have pushed us into the unemployment lines, if you aren't doing anything tonight how about Italian somewhere?"

She kind of expected something like this, she is a nice-looking smart girl that get asked out a lot.

"Thanks Carter, you have always been a very informed help to me back there at work and thank you for that. Tonight, I think I will settle myself, maybe even look at the want ads and check my resumé."

"You are right. Responsibility should be taken care of first. Hopefully, I will see you around town. It was great to work with you, see you."

Pulling into her apartment parking and deciding to leave the coats for now. Grabbing the box out of the trunk, noticed it covered over with a coffee stained shirt, it seemed light for all the things she had, instantly she knew what was going on. Mildly frustrated but happily amused, she left it there in the trunk and grabbed her coats. Getting inside, throwing her things on the couch, poured a glass and waited for the call. Ten minutes later,

"Hello this is Cart...."

"Hi Carter...you are a persistent one and that's good."

"Thank you, I think. Well, it seems that I have mistakenly ended up with all your things, how can I get this back to you?"

"Well, I'm sure you're not the type to go through my personal things, I suppose we could meet tomorrow..."

"But what about all of my training, gather all the intel possible..."

"Dam the Military! Hum, well suppose you could bring it over tonight, if you're so smart do you know where I live?"

"This is the other good part about me, I don't lie. No."

"That is wonderfully encouraging. I'll text a map. You, I'm sure know how to use one of those…"

"And I am sure you have read my file, so you know all things regarding me. Yes. I'll be over in forty-five minutes."

Clapping his hands hard together after making sure the phone was off, he called his favorite Italian for some to-go items and jumped in the shower.

Knocking on appt. 11-C,

"I stand here as proof I really can read a map!"

"Hi again Carter, and yes I smell good things, knew you would bring dinner. But what else goes with Italian?"

"A light Chardonnay."

Having to stop herself midway into correcting him, she looked at him pondering, how did he know she liked white,

"…That's right…"

"Can I pass go?"

"Come on in, set the box down over there on the desk, give me a minute to clear some things here in the kitchen."

Setting stuff down, then moving right into the kitchen sink to help.

"Do you make a swamp, or do you individually sponge?"

"Swamp? What's that?"

"Fill up one side and leave it for tomorrow."

"No, (laughing) I guess that's what Batcheler's do… (fast questioning look) You are a Batcheler aren't you?"

"Confirmed."

"Ok, well good. That's nice of you to help, I'll be honest, this place looks like this most the time. But how about we both sit... Mangiare'!"

"I thought you had a little in you, especially with your beautiful deep chestnut hair."

"Gee thanks, didn't take you long to change from office co-worker to neighborhood rake! (mockingly) Should I be concerned!?"

"Not a bit. You are very safe with me. I like people and I'll be honest; I didn't like the person we used to work for. Thanks for pulling me out of my slump."

In the fold of a few moments realizing strangely, she found herself in a restful peace, a place she hadn't been in a long time. His presence here in her surroundings, didn't concern her. She slowly realized she had completely surrendered to this young man who she has only known for a few months. Sort of absently looking through the different bags that were on the table, glancing at him open the wine, then the high tanging sound of the two glasses. She momentarily worried, was she that dazed? Pulling back into the moment,

"So, thank you for all of this, I thought tonight was going to be all about digging out my resume' and putting all that together. I just realized that I haven't been this relaxed in a long time. So, thanks again."

"We have option's; calzone's x2 or cheese & meet Raviolis for two with a salad. I was going to call and ask, but that would have given my whole plan away."

"I think I was on to you the moment I saw you boxing your things! Ha-ha."

"You didn't give me much choose! Everything kinda had to come together fast!"

Settling into the early evening, the talk turned too who they used work for.

"I know everybody read the message from the 'Long-Distance Associates' and I know he told us absolutely that's all it was. I think I'll call bullshit on all that. I know everybody knew it was something to do with Space. Do you have any other info from your past military career that would put a face on something for sure?"

"Yeah, I do. But I don't want to sound overly dramatic, especially right here now."

"I do appreciate that. But you and I know you said that just to hook me…didn't ya?"

He was poking at some Ravioli that had slipped off his plate,

"Well… maybe. Let's change the subject. How about since we both had Ravioli, we split the…"

Playfully trying to look tuff,

"NO! Humza…this is what I'm thinking; I kept the phone numbers of the people he was always talking about. I'm going to get in-touch with them and see if they want some inside info and guess what…You fell into my trap! I needed someone else from work to back me up! Ha-ha you thought you were making all the moves… and sure, you take one and I'll keep the other…Thank you."

She had a pleased smile on her face, lightly bouncing in her chair and softly clapping her hands.

With a thankful grimness, starting off slowly,

"What part do you have me playing or am I just a box boy. Here's what I am thinking, I imagine we are going to have to move to San Diego and try and work our way in to South Mission Beach, or Borrego Springs. I'm a pilot with deep field experience, also have a degree in Chemistry, but you already know all that."

She paused with a surprised confidant look,

"All right fine. You're a punk and so am I. It's soo nice to meet you!"

They both started laughing and eyeing each other with a little more respect. Sophie had to add quickly with a straight face,

"Don't even think about spending the night here. I'm keeping my guard up with you!"

"Oh, come on now, I wasn't asking... anyway, I can't hang around here, I have to get back home to feed my cat, besides I gotta start packing."

They each let all that soak in for a few seconds.

She almost couldn't believe what she was doing. She stood up pulled the table back a little, sauntered around to his chair and sat on his lap!

Lightly throwing her arms around his neck, only for a hug,

"Man! You are good!"

then moving off around the table and pushing it back where it was. Sitting, resuming dinner and the conversation as if nothing just happened,

"Hope you get use to me."

Carter "Hum, should I be scared?"

"Maybe, one more thing, you better not be with someone now or soon past, or the near future?"

"I told you I don't lie. No. The only future I have planned is with you."

"Good. You're still going home tonight."

Chapter 32

An overpowering defense of emotions and nationalistic self-worth views had been so long instilled in Boxer, that the obvious everyday reality was not visible. Unable to except the latest arrangement, he chose too to fall back on those in high places.

They each in turn didn't see the true motivation of the council's assessment of Boxers performance. He had so softened his side of the story, that of course, some on the military side thought it was a declaration of war. Also of course, the senators were all very diplomatic and thankfully balanced the response to the Moon Council's termination of Boxer.

The response according to the Washington people would come from his pears. Wrongly assuming that they saw Boxer the same way Boxer saw Boxer.

Richard was trying to straighten his basement office/garage, it was freezing all the time in the large open space.

He was building a small space he could heat to do his research, just two walls, a window and a door. Swearing at himself after dropping a big load of 2x4x10' on his foot. That seams always the time that the phone rings…

"Hello Richard, this is Senator Helms. How are you today?"

"Miserable, just dropped a lot of heavy on one foot. How are you."

"Oh my, hope you didn't break anything… An issue has come up and I wanted to ask you about the events on the Moon…"

Immediately going coolly on the defensive,

"What Moon events are you talking about?"

"Well, Mr. Boxer has informed me that you and three others are ambassadors to a Council on the Moon of a sort."

"That's odd, Boxer… who's that?"

"Don't worry Richard all this is ok. We just need you four too talk Boxer up and let the people on the Moon that he's a good fellow and everything is fine. Would you do that for us?"

"Still not sure who and where your Boxer got that from. Let me call you back, my foot is killing me. I am calling a doctor right now."

"Yes, you do that. We'll be in touch."

Hanging up and calling Perla over at the bunkhouse,

"Hay Hun, could you drive me down to the closest Dr. at Harrah's Casino, I think I broke my foot… Auch!!!"

"Ok ok do you need help now or just the car…"

"Just the car would be good…and some water…and maybe a kiss…"

"Oh man you are really hurting, anything stronger, it's a bit of a drive…"

"Just kisses…"

Minutes later she was helping him down all the steps at the observatory, then into the car.

"We have some problems…"

"It's ok I'll go fast but be careful on all the curves, and (kiss-kiss) I'm driving now."

"Your so cute when you're worried."

Perla "Yeah, your nuts. Hay can you call and see if they have what you need, just in case we have to go somewhere else?"

"I will, and I'm a nut for you, yeah I can do that."

Finding that there was infract an Orthopedic Dr. on sight, he then thought too call Wyatt and get everybody on the phone for a conference call on the way down the mountain. Ten minutes later,

Richard "So, this is Boxers latest…"

Alouette "Hay, are you guys are driving somewhere here in town, we can meet you?"

"Nope, Perla is taking me too the Casino for some rework."

Al "Hay now, I want to go!"

Perla "He going to drag this all out, let me fill you in. He broke his foot and I'm taking him to Harrah's Casino Doctor."

Wyatt "What did you do that for?"

"Just wanted attention and some kissing. Check it out, it worked!"

"Ha-ha ok, so do you need us to come up and do something?"

Rich "This is the latest from Boxer. A Senator just called me and told me that Boxer was expelled from the Moon Council and could we put in a good word for him on out next trip. I acted dumb and got off the phone cause of my foot."

There was a small pause, the three had to laugh.

Perla "I can tell that the Senator doesn't know Boxer very well at all, or he is just as crazy. So, I wonder if he's going to drop the lawsuit?"

Alouette "Screw that! I know that makes me look petty, but he broke into our home!"

Wyatt "I'm right with you looking petty, and I don't mind. Also, the bigger picture is what we all are after I know."

Al "Ok, I've got a plan. When you two get all fixed up, your gonna need a place to R & R, so come on down to the beach and hang out for a week or two. What do you say?"

Perla "SOLD!"

Wyatt "We'll have dinner ready, Mexican or Italian?"

Richard "How bout Italian for a change… "

Hours later, with the sun just set, the long-colored lights started painting rippling colors across Mariners Basin. Richard was enjoying comfortably sitting at the dinner table with his new family of interstellar travelers.

"As I suspect that you all will know what I'm going to say…"

Perla "I should hurt myself more often… or some such."

Alouette "Well this worked perfect! We are hosting the best girl in the world too take care of the second luckiest guy!"

That had everyone thinking maybe its coffee time for everyone.

Perla "Took me a sec. You know what, you and I do make an unbeatable Interstellar combination! I gotta change my M O, now it's gonna be the Best Two Girls in <u>this</u> world!"

Everybody toasted to that.

Chapter 33

Combining all their Langley, Virginia apartment furniture, the two new Californians were very surprised to find; the quite beauty surrounding their new home at the Borrego Air Ranch and how easily the two had melted together.

Carter "So I think you are going to girly out our new-to-us place, but don't worry, you can have 60% say in what goes on".

Sophie "Ha-ha, don't you remember our first date at my old apartment? I'm afraid you're gonna get the complete package again right here. You know I'm not a slob, I'm just not overly neat. I get some people to come in and take care of the mess if I get too busy. Speaking to that, I've been meaning to ask, where do you get all your money from?"

"It's nice to know you're not after my cash, but I can ask you the same question you know. As for me, it was a gift from Mom & Dad, a trust. As for the airplane and this place, I actually bought that with some stock sales of 'Berkshire Hathaway."

"Ha-ha that means you only had to sell two shares! What's left?"

"Plenty more. I'm mildly surprised, you and I have been together for only a month and some days, and money has rarely come up. Do you know how refreshing that is?"

"Yeah, Dad left me kind of a lot, I just don't do too much with it now. I used to travel a lot with friends, but I got tired of wakening up with a hangover in a foreign country alone."

"I'll say it, alone...you...hahaha."

"I'm hard to get along with, what can I say."

"I'll say that your picky, and you wait for what you want."

They both sat back, enjoying the sun set over the San Ysidro / Laguna mountain range to the West.

Sophie "I wonder what our unfound friends are doing right now. Wonder if they have time for things like this, I wonder too if you like to hold hands as much as I do..."

"I'll say it, you wonder a lot, and I like it. I think our new unfound friends like to watch the evening fade away.

I know I like a hand that fits comfortably in mine. I like your hands."

"My turn, you like things a lot, and I like that. I like your hand, not too overpowering not too soft, seams just right. I think we will like our unfound friends. I like it here a lot more than the city."

"Ha, I've changed you to a liker instead of a wonderer. I like that..."

Sophie "You are odd. We sound like two characters in a Dr. Suess book! Nicely odd, with a twist of compassion. But If we don't stop complementing ourselves, we are never going to find our unfounded friends!"

They laughed and sat back and filled their glasses and decided on a path.

The next day, Sophie needed some things for the kitchen, so it was off to Center Market. A small, popular, well stocked all around grocery store that serviced this small desert town. They both wanted to get the feel of their new surroundings and this was it.

"Would you stay with me and push the cart while I look for things. Let's see first…"

As he rounded an isle he froze, trying to subtly get Sophie's eye, that didn't work, he pushed the cart into her side,

"Hay man, watch where you're driving."

With a smile she looked at him: he was signaling with his eyes and chin with a whisper,

"It's HER!"

Looking at him kinda sideways,

"What's going on, I'm not getting it…"

He stepped over to whisper in her ear,

"That's Alouette Cantu right there!"

Suddenly, the reason they moved here was real. She slowly turned and yep, that is the black-haired beauty she had seen in the file pictures. She slowly pulled the front of the cart around to another ally then grabbed him and said,

"Go drop something in front of her or bump into her like you just did!"

"No way! Someone that attractive is used to getting picked up. She would blow me off! You gotta do it!"

That made Sophie pull back and reassess her views of Carter in a louder voice,

"So! you think she is so pretty, and that makes you nervous?! What am I chopped liver!"

He started with a smirk, that fell into laughing out loud nervously, and it was contagious, Sophie started in giggling.

Alouette at that time had rounded their aisle, the whole store isn't very large, so things were close together in the first place. As she passed them still laughing,

"Ok, now I have to find out what is so funny?"

That sobered them up fast. Both were trying to come up with something funny – at the same time,

Carter "Well, we just moved here..."

Sophie "We saw all those metal sculptures on the desert, and it reminded..."

That left Alouette with a blank look almost as if she was sorry she asked. That brought Sophie to the rescue,

"Forget it Carter, I'm gonna tell her."

Al's curiosity now was reenergized, but caution mover her off.

"Well ok, how about I'll see you around town later..."

And started to push off with her cart,

"Please wait, my name is Sophie, and this is Carter, we used to work for a Mr. Boxer..."

A turn of her head and hearing that, it was enough to keep her moving off,

Carter "We want to help!"

She stopped, walked back and with a very out of character stern look,

"If you think you can edge your way into our efforts and backstab or undercut us in any way you will be mistaken. Goodbye."

Sophie "I knew she wouldn't believe me."

Alouette had overheard the parting remark, but still carried on her way. She had a few more items to pick up, and this was the easiest market to do it. Making a point to miss the other people along the aisle until the ck-out. Sophie moved so she could be the closest, then talking to Alouette's back,

"I have all his financial records and all of what he is steeling and putting in the Cayman Islands."

That was the magic that turned her. Again, with a very unnatural stern look,

"You then are coming home with me. If for any reason you are lying, you will not like the consequences."

That was all that was said. The two followed Al to her home and were introduced to Wyatt.

"I'm sorry, I don't know if this is going to help or just mess things up farther. These two say they used to work for Boxer and have info on his financial dealings down where we saw him. If not, I told them they would be included in with our lawsuit."

Wyatt a little unsettled and didn't want to invite these new people inside,

"Hello, let's sit out here, it's still morning and cool.

So, tell us, why do you want to help us, or even what gives you the idea we need assistance."

Sophie "Thank you for hearing us out, I was the office manager at his business and Carter was an investigator in my division. I was increasingly concerned with what I would say was very unsound decisions, especially with data, that from what I could tell, made no sense with anything here on Earth. It was the termination of Boxer and the very matter of fact way they presented the situation. I never asked to work with him, it was just more a government annexation of another Senator's work force."

Alouette "I know you can see our worry, I heard you say it at the market. I think we already have a very good case against him, I'm not sure we care to get that involved."

That left a pause,

Carter "Personally, as an investigator I try to explore all things that are available. Knowledge is the key."

Wyatt "You do have a point. Al, you and I have never had to go to a court of this magnitude so maybe let's take a closer look."

Al "My biggest concern is if we are getting sucked into some jacked up backwards plan of that ass!"

That had Wyatt laughing and warning the guests,

"That is highly unusual! If she is using words of that scale... you people better have your shit together!"

That had Al comment,

"And you don't choose words of that nature either, you two really better get it right!"

That left the guests partly relieved, at least they had one thing to check off their list. They talked on into the afternoon a little, then Wyatt through his hands up in the air and stated,

"Too much talk! I'm starved! Let's go to Carmelita's for lunch!"

Alouette gave them the address and asked them to get a table, they would meet them there in 20 minutes.

Wyatt busied himself putting the grocery's away, while Al was off in their bedroom. A few moments later Wyatt was starting to wonder where she went, found her on the Pad with Auch,

"So, they seem ok, I mean is it ok to trust them."

Wyatt came in, sat on the bed with her and made himself known,

"Hi Auch, we are checking up on some new people hope we aren't bothering you."

"That's what I just said funny boy."

Auch "Hello Wyatt, yes I have overheard both of them when they worked in his office and they do not have any back channels that they are trying to establish."

Al "You are so kind thank you. I bought a lot of ice cream for next time you have a moment to stop. Thanks again."

Everybody signed off,

"That was a great idea, thanks!"

"Now that gets all the suspicions out of the way! Let's go ta eat!"

Meeting the two at a table and Alouette sliding in close to Sophie and Wyatt doing the same to Carter, the new kids on the block had very surprised looks,

Alouette "Hi Sophie, sorry I had all those doubts and you also Carter."

Carter "I'm Really glad to hear that. So happy we don't have to turn around now and move back to Virginia."

Al "Wow, you guys did all that, well I hope we can make it worth your while."

Wyatt "If you know all about us then you must know about Perla and Richard."

Sophie "Yes I-we do. I'm new at being we, sorry."

"You guys got married?"

Carter "Um, not quite yet."

Sophie "We honestly just met a month and a half ago; an I haven't scared him off yet."

And so, the afternoon went, it was nice to find new friends that want to help and were fun to be with. It was decided of course not too tell them anything about Auch yet. They did want to introduce them to the others, so they were invited back the following night for dinner at Alouette's.

Alouette wanted to make sure that no one slipped talking around the new guests and keep it simple. The biggest part was getting them out of the house before the 1:00 AM departure time.

Alouette had set a very nice table and tonight it was Wyatt's B-B-Q stake, potato and corn on the cobb.

Perla "I can't imagine having to actually work for that person, that would drive me batty. What else that was odd went on at your old office?"

Sophie "Hum, let's see, when he broke into your beautiful house here and over in South Mission Beach, I was the one who got Richard and Perla out of jail.

Then called the best carpenters and cleaning services I could find, along with the best caters, oh and the limo for jail transport to the beach. Also, for all that stuff up at Palomar Mt."

Al "Au, that was you? Thanks."

Richard "I thank you very much, we did appreciate everything except the jail time."

An enjoyable time was had by all, Carter noticed the framed picture of the two girls flying and invited them up in his twin.

Wyatt "No way! I always wanted to fly a twin! I know Al is going to argue for dibs on first. We always flip quarters to see who's P I C. Where do you keep the airplane?"

"At our place here at the Air Ranch. It's not here yet, a friend of mine is flying it from Virginia, sort of taking his time. Should be here next week."

Richard "All right, not to be nosey but what do you have?"

"Beechcraft King Air 350 i, it's nice for medium long trips."

Al "I think you are in the wrong neighborhood! We can't afford your kind around here! Wow."

Perla "I'm lost, something just passed me?"

Wyatt "I'll say, you are with the wrong crowd, Perla he's referring to a very <u>very</u> nice aircraft. Love to see it someday, now that I know what it is, that's all I will be able to do!"

Carter "All right you guys cut it out, really it's nothing, ask Sophie…"

"I have no idea what is going on right now, something about flying and could I get a refill?"

Perla "I like you! Coming right up!"

Carter talking with everybody,

"See, it's nothing. Me too, if we get invited back, we will bring some suitable stuff along."

Suddenly Wyatt realized it was 12:30! Grabbing Richard and pointing at the clock,

"Hay you know, I want to get up early tomorrow so let's plan another get together time soon."

That clued the other 'travelers' to the time and each one was all of a sudden moving kinda fast. That of course had Carter curious but helping Sophie with a couple of things, they were out the door at 12:45.

"That was really nice didn't you think Carter?"

"It was really nice; I think next time I won't drink so much. Hay you know I think I'm gonna pull over for a little while and sit."

"Yep, me too. But since you're driving, I really don't have any say!"

Moving around the arcing street to a large deserted area, parking and taking out a pair of binoculars and training in on the side doors of Wyatt's home.

154

"What are you up too?"

"I think our new friends have another secret. Did ya think it was a little odd that we got moved out so fast? Let me just watch for ten or twenty minutes, you feeling ok?"

"Yeah, I really like them, I hope this all works out, what do you think you're looking for?"

"At another time you will recall Boxer mention Lono City accidently then trying to cover with another equally bad try Mono City. Saying it was out in the California high desert somewhere. I have a different idea."

"Ok, can I see?"

"Are you asking me?"

"Ha-ha, where are you looking all I see is lights going off like to bed, oh boy that's what I want to do…"

Taking the looking glasses back, he now saw all the lights off and dark figures outlined by the neighbor's night lights. Suddenly, a sloped lit-up doorway appeared floating, the four figures walked into the light, then it went dark. Nothing.

Starting the car, turning around and driving back to the carport. Getting out,

"Hay you stay here, I'm gonna go look at something ok?"

"Sure bet! what are we looking at."

They both quietly got out and without flashlights went over to where he last saw them. Then turned on the lights.

"Look at all the footprints in the sand all together, then they all stop right there! That's all wind-blown natural sand!"

Sophie "That's what I thought! Come on, let's get back home!"

Chapter 34

Things went into overdrive around the desert home,

Al "I sure am glad we packed early! I was having such a wonderful time with those guys."

Perla "Yeah, me too Al, Richard maybe you need to get a pilot's license, ya know so we can hang better with these guys."

"You might be right, but it's time to get out there, Wyatt/Al you need a hand?"

Al "Nope, let's fly, or warp!"

Locking the side doors and making their way single file, seeing the door open, stepping in and each one greeted Auch.

"All set? For your information, your guests are watching you. Would you like to invite them?"

Richard "I think we will wait until next time; it I am sure was going to happen with their amount of interest. Do you guys agree?"

It was unanimous. No surprise, then Richard had an idea,

"Auch could you make a quick jaunt over to their house at the Borrego Air Ranch and …"

"Yes, we are here."

That had everybody laughing briefly,

"I'm going to leave a thank you note, let me wright it before you open the door."

Alouette "Here, leave a bottle of this with it."

Wyatt "Why are we bring Earth wine to the Moon?"

"Because we are meeting Auch's wife remember! You silly!"

With all that done, they found themselves passing through the particle plasma waterfall before they knew it.

"If you feel up to it this afternoon, come on over to my apartment for some dessert like we make it up here."

Richard "We'll be there in 20 minutes."

Each going their ways, later, the Earthlings found themselves at Auch's on the dot.

Auch "Come on in everybody, I would like you to meet Proxy my wife."

Of course, the girls each gave her a big hug and the boys a small peck on the cheek.

Richard "Proxy, your husband has changed so many lives for the better, I am so glad I almost ran over his Space Craft with my motorcycle years ago in the desert. Thank you for giving up your time with him so he can help our fledgling human race."

Proxy "This is wonderful to meet you; he carries on about how much you each have helped him. Come on in and let's sit, what would you like for a after dinner refreshment, we have many different potables, also as you call it, ice cream."

Finding themselves fascinated in the presence of two that had a widely refined understanding of the vast measure of the known Universe and could talk on any subject. The humans found that she personally wasn't broadcasting any condescending nature or pretext of superiority. Talking for a time, they didn't want to wear out their welcome,

Wyatt "You sure are, well, as we say on the planet, 'down to Earth.' Everything is so comfortable here, and Auch certainly has been accommodating in every way. I know Alouette and I would really like to invite you to both too our homes if you ever find a desire too."

Chapter 35

Finding so many things that were coming to mind, Carter let loose with some ideas that he had been holding back, as they headed back to the Air Ranch.

"You remember all that talk about the 'Star Wars Satellite' Protection from Space? Well it's real."

Sophie "Yeah, I know that, nothing new to me, why is that important?"

"They aren't just satellites – they are maned mini stations."

"Really? Why did you tell me that, now that's just one more thing I have to worry about!"

She playfully hit him, as they turned into their drive, stepping out of the car,

"How am I going to sleep tonight with all that info. Hay look, oh boy! Somebody left us more booze!"

Carter grabbed the bottle and the note, opening the door, flicking on the lights and casually glancing at the paper, He froze:

"Holly shit! Check this out! This note is from Richard!"

That had a mildly sobering effect on both,

"Lemesee, Thanks for the fun evening! Will explain in a week. Enjoy!   Ambassador Richard."

Carter "Wow, what did you get me into!"

She playfully hit him again and was hanging on him pulling him down to the couch.

"I am a woman of much Mistry! Be afraid: be very afraid!"

She smothered him with kisses into the good night.

Over the next week they dug back into all the records that Sophie had packed in her legal box when she quit the office. That included thumb drives, calendars and spreadsheets.

"Look at this, every eight weeks he disappeared for a week I don't know why I didn't pick up on that. Now that I know what to look for, over the last year and a half he took four trips down to Grand Cayman."

Carter "Do you know anybody back at the office that you trust to maybe dig deeper. I was no help with spiriting anything out of that place except you."

"Hahum, I'm soo happy!"

"Hay, the airplane in coming in this morning, you want to come with me?"

"Where are you going, we have a runway one block over?"

"Well, you know there's no tower here just a Unicom frequency and it's kinda hard to find if you haven't been here. He's just going to Borrego Springs Airport you know, a couple of miles from here."

"Yep sure, let's go now I'll drop you off come back here and open the hanger for ya. I'll get some Mex from Carmelita's. Then we will figure out what to do."

The new neighbor's airplane made quite a stir among the little aviation community. There are possibly two or three arrivals or departures every other day. Carter's arrival had all the neighbors out on their front porches. (There is a runway along the center of four parallel rows of houses with hangers as their garages for their airplanes. Each house has a radio tuned to 121.5 Unicom to listen to landings and departures.)

Hearing Carter's voice on the radio Sophie casually wandered out to take a look. She didn't have any idea what to expect. A shinny white and chrome twin was on a short final, and overheard the neighbor: That's a Beechcraft King Air 350 i.

To her surprise it was very nice looking, as far as she could tell. Her real fondness was for the guy flying it, she felt a proud wave of affection flowing over her. He taxied around to the back of the house and parked in his own hanger.

She met him after the props spun down with a very big smile,

"I get it. It really is something special."

"You want to go!?"

"Yes. But the stuffs getting cold, and we know Mex doesn't do cold very well."

Setting up an inside lunch, talking things over Carter asked Sophie to come with him to San Diego to drop off Jim. That gave her an idea,

"How about Jim stays here for another day, that way Wyatt and Alouette will be back and oh, how many people fit in your airplane?"

"Our airplane seats 6 comfortably, 8 in a squeeze."

"Au, thanks I always wanted an airplane, anyway we could take them back to San Diego an maybe get to stay at their beach house for a night."

Calling Alouette's cellphone and leaving a very surprised message,

"Ok Show-off's now it our turn to impress you guys, call this number when you get back from, I really can't guess where."

Chapter 36

Richard had a very relaxing week without Ambas Boxer, Acutely, they all did. They found themselves walking more every morning to do a little exploring and of course, Auch and Proxy had dinner with them every evening. Finding all things as they had left them here in the desert, they had Proxy and Auch in for some Earth Pralines & Cream and a tour of their home.

Al "That was just right, the whole week. Back to work, you check your phone yet?"

That queued all the earthlings, each with a rectangle pressed to their head. Alouette had one of interest for all,

"Hay listen to this; (played Sophie's message)"

Wyatt "Hay that would work for us, but I don't think the glider strip FBO rents cars for you two."

Heading East out of the Air Ranch, then making a slow turn back West, their climb out was so fast the cleared the mountains with ease.

Wyatt "The last time I took off from the Borrego Airport I had to circle up for ten minutes. This is really nice!"

Of course, Al & Wyatt flipped for the co-pilot seat. He promised he would turn it over to her next time.

Al "You don't want to be up front on you first flight?"

Sophie "I'm kinda new to flying at this scale, we went the day we got it. Until I know a little more about flight dynamics I'll sit back here, besides this is really nice."

⁜

It was Sophie & Carter's turn again to be overly impressed with their other home at the beach.

"This is perfect!

Finally, with people they could talk with,

Wyatt "Ok now down to business. We have a lot to cover. We will fill the details at another time. Since Perla and Richard aren't here, whatever is discussed they are part of also.

We are Earth's Ambassador's to the Moon."

That naturally dropped jaws and added questions that were answered with,

"Later. Let's get through the intro first!"

That took a while, dinner and a walk up to the ocean boardwalk for the sunset still had more questions than answers.

Alouette "Now, it's important we get all our facts together for the legal action. Most importantly the six of us must produce a plan of action that will convince all of Humanity that they have friendly neighbors! Easy!! Right?"

En todo started laughing.

Wyatt "I truly hope we can keep this attitude through the entire awakening. Hope relates to love. We have thru-out human history reacting into the unknown with too much hostility. It's a basic human response that we must some way turn around."

Al "Our first idea, as a start, was this court business. We are countersuing for Breaking and Entering, plus some other things."

Carter "B&A isn't by itself really anything, I can say that he has more of a case. All he needs to do is introduce the phrase 'National Security' and it will be all over for you.

These days just saying that fraise can put your case with the FBI, CIA and then you're done. We've got to get him on a similar charge, that would in some sense level the playing field."

That let everybody think for a moment,

Sophie "How about stealing federal moneys?"

Carter "That would defiantly work. I overheard you way back at the market tell Alouette that you had bank records from somewhere in the Caribbean."

Al "We also saw him with a girl that I am sure wasn't his daughter. How far do your records go back?"

"I think I have 2 years maybe. It's all on thumb drives, no paper. I have Bank receipts from Grand Cayman, also the expense report for all the trips."

Wyatt "I think that we should get in touch with the attorneys and present all we have. Next time we go to the desert I'll remember to bring all our records back here; I know Richard & Perla have already done that."

Sophie "I have all my thumb drives here; it you want we can make copies."

"Great! Between all the laptops I think we can get things done. Then dinner in P B somewhere."

All were happy with that.

Chapter 37

Mr. Boxer was trying his best, but it had been so long he really didn't know what that was. Trying to arrange work people, new office staff and computer deliveries was not going well. Tossing frustration to the wind,

"Is there someone here that was hired as an office manager? How about you, that's your job now. Get this all settled fast! I need order!"

There were eleven people coming and going in this large room with confused looks on their faces. The one person that Boxer was singled out did do one thing, she quit.

Boxer alone in his office gave his lieutenant a call,

"Any luck with contacting Lono City?"

"Yes, they still say they will deny our ship from landing. I can't find any other way in."

Chapter 38

Alouette was a little nervous sitting in the witness box. It was decided to put all the facts out there to possibly flood the jury with information.

Wyatt had previously outlined all his involvement with Auch over the two and a half years he has known him.

"All the information that we were given form Auch was purely for the advancement of our human condition. Do you realize right now as we speak, there are two thousand people living in the Moon? They have always been there. A very kind and peace-loving people. They are very concerned about all our wars, hate and violence. Our neglect with not taking care of our Earth home is very high on their list."

At this point the judge put a stop to everything.

"The Jury in total will disregard all that the last two witnesses have stated. This matter will now be moved to a higher federal court."

The attorneys had anticipated this, Wyatt and Alouette had no idea what was going on.

"Your honor, we have infallible uncompromising evidence we would like to present to you in your chamber."

Judge "Denied. Court adjourned."

With the slam of the gavel, that was that. Maybe.

The judge immediately entered his chamber. Starting to disrobe, he heard a voice behind him, turning,

"You are breaking the law; I'm calling the bailiff!"

"That will be fine."

The judge stopped and looked at the man, his appearance was unusual, something wasn't quite right.

"Who are you?"

"My name is Auch. I will say you are making things harder on yourself. My suggestion is to call the bailiff and call court back in session. If you don't take me seriously, I will turn your world upside-down."

"Yes, good make-up."

At that, Auch turned the whole room upside-down, with the judge standing on the ceiling. With all the furniture still on the floor. Very casually Auch walked over to the befuddled judge and steadied him,

"This is nothing. Would you like more real facts like this to convince you?"

With all the yelling going on the bailiff did rush in to make sure the judge was ok. Seeing him and another man walking on the ceiling, that seemed to freeze him. The judge called out,

"Get me down!"

Auch then righted the situation,

"I suggest another session of the same court start now."

The judge staired at Auch with indecision, that prompted Auch too flip the room once again, this time with the bailiff. All three now upside down, again Auch steadied both men.

"We can stay like this if you like…"

"Ok-Ok fine."

Auch putting everything right, the judge passed an order to the bailiff.

"Call the last session back in order, quick! And tell no one about this!"

The judge turned to question the intruder, but he was gone.

Auch left the chamber, now with his glasses on, he took a seat with the new session audience to be sure it was going in a propped direction.

To say it was highly unusual is an understatement. The jury was most difficult to heard back together, some were frightened some just wanted to get back to work. But all had to admit, it was interesting.

"All rise: Court is now back in session."

Alouette was very confused sitting back in the witness box,

"Again, as I was saying, everything that Wyatt and I have stated is true. As to the reason we mentioned this with this case of Breaking and Entering is because Mr. Boxer was abusing his authority on many levels, destruction of federal property and still is stealing Federal money. We have printed evidence along with my personal witness of Mr. Boxer in a Grand Cayman Bank. There is nothing to be afraid about form our interstellar neighbors. The only thing you must be cautious about, is people in high places here on Earth that try to tell you that the aliens want to hurt us. That is a lie. A question for you? All of you here right now, do you feel threatened?"

It took a few seconds, but people started shaking their heads "No."

"I am telling you they are so much like us, so much so in every way, I'll bet you wouldn't believe me if I told you that one is with us right now."

That had most people looking around, and muttering, the judge hit his gavel a little over hard,

"Order! Order here now. The new evidence I recently witnessed has rearranged my views differently, and this court will now hear views on the subject."

After court, they strolled back to their offices, Auch walked with them from the courthouse and had a comment,

"Alouette I must say, you had me on the edge of my seat, as you say here."

"Ha-ha, well I know you don't want to be called out, I wouldn't do that. I didn't expect you to be there at all, but I'm really glad you were. I tell ya, Wyatt and I were really on edge ourselves after the first session was stopped. We didn't know what we were going to do."

Wyatt "All I could think of was the Fed's coming after us, I was thinking about buying the apartment on the Moon~!"

Alouette "That's a great idea! Can we Auch?"

"I have a feeling that Wyatt is joking. Of course, we can make arraignments if you are not. Yes, the attorneys and I had made preparations without your knowledge, we didn't want you to rely on my appearance in the judge's chambers."

All things at Court were thrown into another 'Discovery phase' so next Court date was in 6 months.

Chapter 39

Of course, Carter and Sophie had been hinting at meeting Auch, and it was their turn to host a dinner so,

"Now that we are all here and as far as I know- Don't have to meet up with someone at 1:00 AM... I'd like you ask a favor of the four of you; can we get a ride on Auch's machine?"

Nobody was taken by surprise, that is, until Richard asked Carter & Sophie,

"I'm sure that would be ok, if...you agree to one thing."

Sophie "And that one thing is?"

"You must commit too being Ambassador's from Earth to the Moon."

That took the host and hostess by complete surprise, never expecting anything like this,

Carter "Wow, ah, I can answer for myself..."

Sophie "And I can answer for both of us, Yes!"

The next night at 1:00 The group quietly walked on the soft scrunchy sand, two of the six were taking in all the visual and physical que's possible. On this night with no moon glow spread over the desert, they were last in the line entering the craft, with the only thing visible was a bright curving slope of a doorway.

"Welcome Sophie, welcome Carter, my name is Auch. I am sure there questions but let's get on the way."

The two were given the two seats closest to where Auch sat at the control shelf.

"You will feel a small one-G pull holding you on Earth, then take note of the aft and forward view screens."

Perla had taken note of Sophie's interest in the control shelf and explained over her shoulder,

"The layout of all the controls are only visible to him. Most control of the craft is telepathic, theirs only a few things he does physically. Check out the Earth get small, now look at the Moon get big…fast!"

Wyatt "Carter check out this landing, I never get tired of this plasma waterfall."

Now, trying to pull everything together so fast, they both were realizing that this was the Moon, and this is the wall of a creator, and yes it did look like flying into a waterfall! The view screens went dark and the door slid open,

"Welcome to Lono City! Watch your step, now, we will meet in twenty minutes. I will leave you in the capable hands of Richard, he will show you to your apartment."

Still in shock and responding to the welcome with not much more than Wow, thank you, wow! Richard herded the group onto a G-cart and gave the new commers a tour of what was available.

"We will get into all this after we get settled, when we get to our rooms, be ready for another "only at the movies" moment."

Arriving in the garage with view,

"Each of you, just place your thumb here in the rectangle and that will be your method of privacy."

After entering the apartments, Richard calling out,

"Hay… Maud!"

From around the corner, a small floating robot appeared.

"Welcome Sophie and Carter, if you would follow me, I will show you to your rooms. And welcome again: Alouette, Wyatt, Perla and of course Richard."

Carter "Really?! This is way past what I imagined!"

Richard "If you two need more time, we can take the tour later, just tell Maud, she knows all about you, so go for it."

The new kids were on their way, the timeworn kids split up and got themselves settled.

Ten minutes later everybody was out front stepping into the larger G-cart with Auch. Comfortably taking the same tour of the United Galaxy's meeting hall and answering very similar questions from Sophie and Carter. Dropping them all off at the Common area for a late moon dinner.

"Have a good evening, don't forget to walk back to your apartment."

Richard "Yeah we do walk a lot up here, come on, let's relax for a while, we'll get a rim table and order."

Sophie "You guys, I really hope they have booze here…"

That question fueled their laughter that turned the heads of some of the other 'people' there at the newly named 'hole-in-the-wall' restaurant.

"Yes they do! It is soo much better than that stuff on Earth, I brought Wyatt & Al here when they first arrived, Wyatt came up with the name. Alouette also has some creative names for some of the food & drinks I think you will enjoy, let's step in!"

At the end of the week, the newcomers had found they made a very nice impression on the other ambassadors in the United Galaxy's chambers. It was mentioned a number of times that they were very pleased the 'other' person was no longer present.

Stepping out of Auch's craft into the warm night, Alouette had invited Auch in again for some desert dessert. He had an idea he wanted to present.

"Carter from what I have learned about your past, it seems that you were involved with a large number of classified investigations.

"Yes, I have been sent into some very odd places. I discovered that once they find out that you are good at something, they keep asking again and again. I started to feel like I had dodged too many metaphoric and real bullets, and maybe my time was getting thin. So I bowed out. Why do you ask?"

Auch "My thoughts are just that, thoughts… but I think a look at Mr. Boxers business holdings…"

Sophie "I think I just found my new place here on Earth. I know how that person thinks and what direction he wants to go. We could head back to Virginia and rent a place for a while and you could do the things you like to do."

"I have a question; I think I mentioned that I don't like to get shot at. How did 'like' fit into any to this?"
"Oh so easy! I won't send you to places that shoot at you!"

Everybody kinda smiled, but it wasn't very reassuring. Thankfully Auch had some other thoughts.

"I believe I can assist you in some areas that don't violate the code that I must abide by, you can be easily made 'built proof.'"

Right off the bat, Richard knew exactly what Auch was talking about.

"I got it! The Gravity Stick!"

"Yes, that's the one, I think that will be fair enough."

Carter and Sophie, looking at each other had no clue what was going on,

"A Gravity Stick?"

Rich "Would you like me to go grab it?"

"No, I will, presently, I would like to finish my dessert first. Let's talk some more regarding your move. We must consider A location that is easy for you to 'visit' different locations that Boxer surly is involved with. The most important one, is a location that I can park my craft without notice."

Alouette was carefully listening to all this and something just struck an odd cord,

"Can I stop everybody for a minute. We need to think about each one of our wants and needs, we all are giving up a lot! Someday; I personally want to start a family, and yes, I personally want to bring the Earth in line with the rest of the Galaxy. Those are two ginormous desires! We really have just met you two and we are asking you to move right back where you started without much thought. I know, because I am guilty of it, I really like how thing are moving so fast, it seems we are getting things done. But we can't forget about 'us.' The same with you Perla and Richard, you gotta think about each one of yourselves. And one more thing, how can we afford all this, our business is a research grant funded effort with not much breathing room. I hate to be a Debby Downer..."

Auch "A Debby Downer? I'm not familiar with that colloquial reference."

That was enough to lighten the room with a little laughter, but Al's thoughts were definitely taken into close consideration.

Carter "Thank you Alouette, I-we are just getting to know each other and yes, you are right, everything is moving fast. As for me, I am entering a time in my life that I'm very sure I don't want to change in any way."

Sophie "Yep! Me too, this guy doesn't know it yet, but he ain't going anywhere without me!"

"I don't intend to ever let you too far out of my sight. As far as moving for a time, I'm fine with that, also in regard to the financial side of things, we're good."

Sophie "Yeah, I'm good on the financials too. As far as everything moving the way it is now, I like it. Thank you Alouette and Perla you bring in a warm personal side, thanks for your concern."

Auch "Now that you have brought finances up, I understand there might have been an omission in my presentation of ambassadorship. The appointment is a paid position and you each have an account in Lono City. Your thumb print is your passbook and you are able to withdraw US dollars at any time. I will make arraignments when I return tonight for a deposit to be made into each of your accounts here on Earth."

Chapter 40

One week later, the East coast sure felt cold, compared to where Sophie & Carter had been. They were just getting use to their new desert home.

Reston, Virginia was their next address right next door to a country club with a lot of wooded and open space. It was a bigger place than they wanted but it was just for a short time. Auch took a moment to visit after they had settled in, it was more of a practice run.

It was late evening and they were expecting a visitor. "Auch wow! This is fantastic! How was the approach, I know we are close to all the big things, D.C. & CIA is just down the road 10 or so miles. Come in and have a sit, I have my own East coast kind of dessert if you like…"

And so it went for an hour or so, as he was leaving, he gave something to Carter,

"This will keep you perfectly safe, what is your weight at present?"

"Oh about 220 plus or minus."

"Alright, this is set for only you. If Sophie or someone else is with you, you must change this setting x-2 very easy. The next thing is you must be in physical contact with who you are trying to include! Do not forget. When you are alone, remember to keep your arms and legs close together. Walking is fine, but in a fast run you may extend the coverage."

"Well I certainly thank you!"

"Oh yes and do remember to take the x-2 off, if you don't you will float away."

That had both of them wanting to try,

"I'd like to try it out before you leave, so I now am setting it for one... now."

Pushing the wand button did nothing that he could tell, until Auch through his dessert fork directly at Carter's head, and he flinched! The fork easily glanced off,

"Wooo, I didn't feel anything, now Sophie let me try the x-2 key."

Doing that she hugged him: and Auch through another fork at the two, and nothing. Then Carter let go of Sophie and he did start to float towards the ceiling.

"Now you must be careful once you press the off key, you will drop from what ever height you have ascended too. You must push off something to send yourself back down earthward."

Thanking Auch and walking him out to his craft,

"This is the best we could find in a hurry, hope it works for you."

"Yes. This is a better location than the desert, here the tree cover is thicker, and I don't suppose too many people play golf at night. Thank you for dessert, and I will see you in three weeks."

Now with everything set in place, Sophie had to start digging into what was left of Boxers office.

"Tomorrow I'm going to go the office and ck out the lay of the land so to speak. Maybe even drop of one of the bugs that you have left over from working for the very same person!"

Carter "What gave you the idea that I have anything like that?"

"You are an investigator, aren't you?"

"Yeah but we all don't just have a stock issue of handguns, tazzers, brass knuckles and listening devices."

"Yes you do. Remember I was your office manager and that means I saw everything that was purchased, rented or stollen."

The next morning they both walked into their old office and were greeted with blank faces.

"Well you two look happy, what's you secret? Don't bother I know the answer, you got another job with people that have a sole, right?"

"Ha-ha yes you can say that! Nice to see you, so how's my old job treating you?"

"Not too bad, it's just when he's around that things get strained, what brings you two back here?"

"I think I left a couple of things in the break room."

Carter "and I am just tagging along for the ride, I think I'll go say hi to a couple of guys over in the low rent investigating area."

Each moving off in different directions around all the cubbies. The plan was to put a bug in Boxers office and one in Carter's old area. That was easy but getting one into his main office was going to be difficult. After the break room she headed for his office. The plan was, Carter was supposed to talk up the O M while Sophie slipped into his office and put one in the bookshelf. Doing that, she noticed one of her own books and decided to take it. On the way out, the office Manager mentioned she wouldn't say anything about Sophie going into his office.

"Oh, I remembered I lent him this book, ck it out, there my name stamped inside the cover. Hope you all hang in and I just gotta say, I hope he puts salt instead of sugar in his coffee."

On their way out, Carter had to comment,

"He put's salt in his coffee? That's all you could come up with, ha-ha, salt in coffee, your just cruel and mean spirited. I'm surprised we ever got together!"

"I couldn't think of anything else you goofball! I didn't want to say anything really mean. So glad I ran across the book!"

"Goofball! now I think we have to break up! I have never been insulted that professionally before!"

She lightly wacked him, and arm in arm they pulled each one closer to the other one.

Chapter 41

Downtown San Diego was feeling very seasonal, getting ready for the Summer to end and School too start. Fall colors on the few deciduous trees between all the palm trees scattered across the town. It's just about all the seasonal change you get here in so-cal. Alouette was looking out her office window, watching mom's and their children moving along the sidewalks from store to store. Wyatt quietly walked in behind her,

"Everybody getting ready for school, that's always great for the stores but I can tell, you're thinking about kids..."

"Yes I am."

"Hum, that sounds like very certainly absolutely yes. What are you gonna do about it?"

Al "I might lock my door and jump your bones!"

"I have a better idea, let's find some place on the Moon with less gravity and try it!"

That gave her pause, thinking,

"That means you want to start too! It all so means that you wonder about the same thing as I do, what's it like with nothing holding you down?!"

"And that means that your just as weird as I am!"

Laughing and hugging, they both staired out the window thinking of their next visit to the Moon...

Chapter 42

Virginia in this fall season was your typical 'riot of colors' with leaves lingering on trees and giving the walkways & gutters a much-needed wrapped-in earthy softer colorful look. Carter at the moment was swearing at those same leaves for making so much crunchy noise!
He was attempting to get into Boxers house and reciprocate in a nice way by placing some listening/viewing devices. He was talking to Sophie on his earphone,

"I can hear the leaves crunch from here! I thought you were 'sneaking-up' on this guy."

"Very funny, you just keep your eye on his cellphone locater and tell me when he drives up here. You have the alarm co. blocked yet?"

"Just getting that done, ok you only have 15 minutes, remember I can't do this trick twice in on night."

"Got ya, at the side door lock… I'm inside now, heading for the office. You sure about the alarm I still see lazors in the office."

"Yeah, sez so here."
Seeing the concentration of beams exactly Infront of the safe with the tint glasses he was wearing,

"This safe is as older then dirt. This should be easy, keep me posted on the time."

"Have you lost your manors, please and thank you don't forget…"

"Ok, please be quite."

Watching the listening device screen spike up go flat, spike up go flat a number of times, he soon opened the door.

"I'll scan as many as I can until I run out of time with the alarm. Let me know about anybody driving up...please."

"Ah, that's more like it. Your welcome. How much stuff is there?"

"A lot! Can't do it all in one, there's some pictures here of him and a bunch of military saucers with hundreds of Grays! They don't look very alive, I gotta get this. Let me know the time thank you."

Getting himself back to his place, he plugged in and downloaded what he found with Sophie,

"This is all budget figures for the Moon base and for – I don't know if this is right, manufacturing of 'Alien troops' I don't know what that means, you say there's a lot more of the same kind of thing?"

"Yes, this has a very familiar ring to it. I for one, know this has been in the works since before the Viet Nam war, False Flag operations."

"What are you talking about, I know computers really well and I don't recall hearing or seeing anything like that."

"It doesn't really have anything to do with that stuff, it's all about a one world order. One of the ways to do that is fake a war with the Aliens, then rally the World around one common goal. The very rich from here and it doesn't matter what other country, want to control the world, and the number of how many people there should be. There are some so Psychotic, they honestly believe that starting a US – Russian nuclear war will bring back Jesus, and that will begin the new world order.

 If there was anything left. There are some Generals in the pentagon right <u>now</u> that would start that war yesterday if they could!"

"Oh come on your just being a negative reactionary, people are good! They wouldn't do that; I suppose you are one that thinks that the Muslims weren't involved in New York."

"They had nothing to do with it. I can show you someday, and all the things that are already orbiting the Earth, but let's not get sidetracked right now. We need to help Wyatt & Al, we have to find a beginning to all this so we can help let the world know that our neighbors are friendly, ya wanta?"

Sophie "Ok, well, I was going to tell you to put salt in your coffee…"

"You what! That's it! We are over!"
As he fell into her, pushing her onto the couch, smothering her with kisses…

Chapter 43

Richard and Perla were combing over some new data from the Moon to add it into the record.

"Ya know, we could probably just push a button somewhere when we are up there next time and get a better readout."

Perla "Well, how would that look on the logbooks from Earth, data entry: Location – Moon, I was just there. I think there are some people who still don't believe we even made it to the Moon, let alone a city inside the Moon. If we told just about anybody that we go there for a week every eight weeks, they would think that we had lost our marbles!"

"Yeah, but it sure would be easier."

Perla "You know, it's downright boring now that Auch doesn't stop by anymore. What do you think about getting a place down around those guys. We could move out of the Bunkhouse, our time here is almost done."

Richard "I'd rather get a place down around south mission beach, but I know we couldn't afford it. Let's think about it, your right we should find a place soon. All our contract work for Wyatt & Alouette's company is really done."

The hunt was on, (for a house) and it didn't take long, they landed on renting Carter & Sophie's place until they return from the East coast.

"It's gonna be great! I can park my motorcycle right next to Carters toy! Hay, have you ever been riding? I'll get one for you!"

Perla was sitting back and letting him verbally dream about things she had no intention doing.

"No thank you. Maybe I'll get my pilots license over at Borrego Airport while you're busy bouncing over the desert."

Chapter 44

Stepping into Auch's interstellar craft, Perla mentioned,
"Hay aren't Sophie and Carter coming on this week's outing?"

Auch "Yes, I thought you would want to see their new home in Virginia."
That had them from the California desert to Reston, Vi in less than one minute. Stepping out they all had a small home tour and then on their way to the Moon.

Wyatt "Carter, we want to thank you for getting all those printouts, it should go a long way."

"That's nothing my next visit is going to be his office, thank god it's not in CIA headquarters proper. That will be where the real direction of things should turn up."

Auch "You will be busy this week with mining exports/imports to planets in my home galaxy. Also there are some members that would like you, Richard to show them the exact location and what was discussed with the Ex-Ambassador. They are also presenting a case against Boxer."

Richard "I really do hope this doesn't turn into a case against Earth in general. This doesn't sound good."

Auch was reassuring but even as they splashed through the plasma waterfall Richard was now wondering if these were some of the groups he'd been warned about.

Getting settled, Richard felt he needed to talk with everyone in a relaxed place, walking over to 'Hole in the wall,' the place with the nonstop view of the large creator, Earth and the stars beyond.
Finding a lonesome table at the window,

"Do you remember when Auch gave us that talk about other civilization's having undesirables, with reference to our own group of not so desirables types like Boxer."

Perla "No, but I think you told me about that after it happened, that was a long while ago, I think it was just Wyatt and yourself."

"Yeah, I remember that. What's got you thinking so much?"

"Auch isn't being as forthcoming as he usually is and he is talking about this week's schedule, Alnitak system, Zeta Orionis his home planet, he sounded worried, I've never noticed that before, have you guys?"

Al "Yes, I'm glad you brought that up Richard, he seemed a little out of sort all the way here, all ten minutes of it, ha-ha."

Richard "Maybe I'll stop by his place tonight after we're finished here. Maybe he'll open up too just one person."

Perla "I have an idea! Proxy, gave me her pad number. I'm calling her now; anyone know what time it is on Zeta Orionis?"

That thankfully broke the serious fog over the group, just enough to order some dinner. While that was in the works,

"Hello Proxy, this is Perla, Richards friend…"

"Yes Perla, I almost expected a call, I can see you are all there, He won't say anything to any of you but an old acquaintance of his is starting a troubling situation. Very simply: making a large issue out of a small one."

"How can we help."

"I think with the six of you in session, make a standing uniting effort for friendship and harmony between the peoples of the Moon and Earth. It seems Mr. Boxer has poisoned a number of delegates feelings, even one particular one from our home planet here. It seems you have a double purpose: one of convincing the inhabitants of your planet, and the other; convincing the inhabitants of the Moon. I said at the start that it was a small issue, and it is to a wide majority. There is always contrary dissenting voice, born out of misunderstanding of a balanced way of thinking. I will say this; the positive energy that all of you bring to any gathering will be of an enormous help to Auch."

The discussion carried on for some minutes with a better thankful understanding of a direction to follow. The after dinner walk back, ended up at Auch's front door.

Richard "Hope we aren't disturbing, won't take long." They were invited in and Perla lead off with,

"I just got off the pad with Proxy, we noticed that you were a little quite on the way up here."

"She just called. It never was my intention that you now, not only have to convince Earth that all is mostly well, now you must do the same with our people here. I truly wasn't intending, nor did I anticipate the negative reaction and the bad taste that Boxer left with my peers."

Wyatt "I think we might just turn this into a learning situation for both peoples. What I mean is; how about a small group of dissenting detractors from each, the Earth and the Moon and we swap places. Of course we won't call them that, they could see how the United Nations works, and vice-versa. Then on to other countries and let them choose wherever they want to go. They could end up in a prison, a business or the military wherever they would like to go and ask questions of the people there. It might take a long while, and this just came to mind; do you have prisons here or on any of your other planets?"

He actually had to pause and consider before he spoke,

Auch "No, none here. None on my home world, but as I have said before there is a aggressive element in some other civilizations, and they are interplanetary."

"But you said in the past, that they must abide by the Galaxy wide mandate too not interfere with developing planets, right?"

"Yes that is correct. They would be deemed hostile and could be deleted."

Richard "Wo! As in obliterated, gone, not there anymore?!"

"Yes. You find that excessive?"

"Yeah, kind of, don't you think so?"

"No. When dealing with a burgeoning planet in such a way that changes the entire planet to benefit a small group of beings is not tolerated."

Wyatt "Um, first of all, is that possible? I mean can you really erase mass groups?"

"Yes. It would be decided by the counsel that you all are part of. It obviously doesn't happen that much anymore, and the statues-que of the Galaxy is much improved."

Perla "Wow, so there really is a Death Star?"

Auch "My turn to laugh at myself, no, nothing like Star Wars. My children really like the movies, it is nice to hear them laugh so hard at so many things in the movie.

The judgement is carried out by eliminating all of the offending beings interstellar transportation. A minimizing of their import/export trade and expelled from the Galaxy of Nations for fifty years."

Alouette "Oh, that's not so bad."

Auch "It really is; for a Race to lose the interstellar possibility's is like removing their legs. It would be as if all of your automobiles were taken away."

Richard "Your right, that is bad, but it isn't as bad as I first thought. It was the word deleted, in reference to the being no longer among the living. Ok, let's get on with here and now. Anybody else have other ideas please put it out there."

Auch "My apologies, I am still learning your ways. Yes to here and now. It's getting on and you will need to be in full attendance tomorrow. Let's meet again tomorrow for dinner in the dome."

That suited everyone, on the walk back it was decided that they would put a plan forward like Richard had outlined. Back at their apartment, they started an outline and immediately ran into trouble,

Al "How do we choose 'cautious detractors' from each location. It can't be military or political who would really believe them! How are we going to find someone that can convince a large group of people?"

Perla "How about movie Hollywood types?"

The rest of the group,

"No way, nope!"

"Ok, ok how about artists, or even rock stars? You gotta remember we don't have to convince the young people; they are going to really dig it. Especially if someone they follow say a lot of positive stuff about our neighbors. It's the old religious people that are going to flip out!"

"Hum, now you might have something there Perla. What do you think, we could get some on the highbrow side and whoever is popular now in the rock world. Oh, and of course Father O'Neal!"

That gave everyone a smile, and off to bed for all.

On the following day, some attention was expected, but not at the level they had supposed. There were some delegates that had an obvious distrust in the humans, but there was a far larger following of supporters.

It was decided that a review of the areas that Boxer had shown to Richard would undergo a review of physical intent, to be sure there was no development above or below the surface.

A group of four surface hovering craft, that looked like mini vans, with no wheels had Richard dutifully showing a group to the crater in question. Finding nothing above, and according to the geo x-ray, nothing below was detected.

That night at dinner Alouette had a question,

"Auch, is there any one person or group that a large segment of the population is interested in, or take opinion with? What I am looking for is roughly like your entertaining personalities, like we have on Earth."

"Well not really, most everybody here is involved with making a positive, meaningful and I must add, honest contribution to society."

That had everybody laughing,

Alouette "Yes, there is way too much of 'I want to be just like all the people in Hollywood' syndrome covering the entire world! Entirely too many people sitting and not doing! Ok, sorry off my rant, Auch you know what we are trying to do, and yes, we will probably enlist some of those 'Hollywood types' to aide us."

"I think some of the very detractors you met today night be in amongst some other notables that I will suggest. One more amendment; including any military is of the highest risk I can think of. Not truly knowing where their heart or intentions may truly lie."

Richard "I wonder, and I don't know why we haven't asked about this yet, what happens when there is an aggressive intruder here. Who goes out to fight?"

Auch "You do. If something of that nature happens it goes before an emergency counsel, you vote on it and it's done."

Wyatt "So I'm guessing someone somewhere, would press a button and that would be that?"

"Yes, of course there would be a routine warning, and if they still advance, they are invalidated. Or as you would say, blowen-up... Actually in our case, we would create a negative zone at the midst of their mix, and they would be imploded, they would collapse in on themselves. That would save the rest of the solar system from any large dislodged debris."

Alouette "Wow, and people on Earth think we could win a war with our interstellar neighbors. I get so disgusted with people in power on Earth."

Auch "Let's think about what you just said, people in power... That sounds like your talking about people that are far above you, untouchable. Seems to me, you each have that same power here. You are in the very seat of what you're talking about: you can put forth ideas here that could start a beginning somewhere else. You need to use your leverage to motivate here first. Remember, I can not inform you exactly how or what to act on."

That had the group finishing dinner in a introspective mood. Still a lingering question came to mind,

Wyatt "Can we assemble a group here talk to leaders from a number of nations in a secret location. What I am guessing is transporting world leaders all to one location, that also would include the ultra-rich individual's in Europe. Introduce each other and explain that the world they live in is nothing like the everyday world of regular people worldwide. This now, is the <u>real</u> world, something they are so out of touch with they must keep all their religious preference's too themselves for a time.

But for now, all of Earth gets introduced to their interstellar neighbors. We will worry about the fossil fuel people losing their minds later."

Perla "And the religious people losing their minds before the oil people do..."

Alouette "Remember the Vatican announced that there is no issue to existing church doctrine with the inclusion of ETB's. The Vatican astronomer said Christians should consider alien life as an "extraterrestrial brother" and a part of God's creation. I think that was in 2012."

Auch "I think you might be on the right path, that's all I can say."

The balance of the week did start to sway away from the Earthlings and did move into mining and trade balances, but on Thursday, Richard brought everything back to a Earth focus.

"Members of this distinguished counsel, I would like to propose a board of consideration into the selecting of a team of representatives from surrounding planets. The goal is too present ourselves to the world leaders in a one time, single select location, with the intention to make all the peoples of Earth know it's neighbors currently in the Galaxy. The quantity and likely individuals chosen will be determined by the discovery board. I request a vote now; yes or no, from the Ambassador's present."

The aggregate positive response was overwhelming and so they continued to appoint board members from eight of the closest interstellar planets to Earth. At the next gathering in eight weeks, the board would convene too elect representatives from this body on the Moon, to the planet Earth.

Chapter 45

On the return trip back to Earth, Sophie had asked Auch to stop in at their desert home to pick up a couple of items before heading over to the East coast.

Auch did an invisible hovering search of the house and found more listing devices.

"Would you like to do away with these devices as we have done in the past at Wyatt's home?"

Wyatt "Hay let's collect them and use that as more evidence at court."

Alouette "Can we just knock them out and not melt them? They smell so bad for a long time!"

Doing that and then getting the East coast couple safely home, Auch was mentioning to Carter and Sophie, hovering in their back yard,

"It seems Mr. Boxer doesn't mind replacing mainframes and the labor that goes along with it. You folks have acquired a few bothersome listening devices of your own, would you want them likewise taken care of? (Yes please.) I am aware of your next two places of hopeful unnoticed entry, please let me know it I can help with any legal assistances, otherwise the best of luck. Good night you two!"

It wouldn't due to have any video of his presence at his old place of employment, so Carter, of course had made a double set of keys before he left. Being an investigator had taught him to plan for the unexpected, they should have changed out all the locks, but you never know. The office was located a few blocks off the DC Mall and had a medium amount of security.

Knowing full well that the hard keys were just a start: there was a couple of Fob swipes that needed special attention. Normally when high end employees quit, the office manager changes over the locks and passwords.

Getting into the building via the reception area and stepping into the storage/broom closet there was one thing he always thought odd. Almost all offices had a drop ceiling with 2'x4' or 2'x2' cellulite ceiling tiles that are easily lifted and pushed aside with the tough of a finger. Granted the space is small, he had brought along some items that would help get him through, also making him appear to be a maintenance man if need be.

Care must be taken to place the 1"x 6" x 6' boards on the main load barring 'i' beam ceiling runners, but he wasn't in a rush. It's always a bother with A/C duct work in the way but he finally made it to Sophies old office, and this was the hard part.

Chousing a spot with one of the 4" fire sprinkler supply lines parallel to the ceiling, then moving the ceiling tile aside, from a semi crawl grabbing the iron pipe and pulling himself out over the open space in the ceiling, dropping to the floor. Rising from a crouch it hit him,

"What the hell am I doing!"
Reaching in jacket and pulling out the gravity stick and turning it on, he adjusted the digital weight scale to one-pound heavier

than his weight. Switching it on, he lifted off the ground six inches.

"What a dumb-shit, ok let's readjust the 'G-stick' and see about the locked file cabinet and stop talking to myself."

Making his way too Sophie's desk, he had a quick passing thought, 'Hay, I remember a pretty girl that used to sit here.' Then just as fast back to attaching the electronic mag-destabilizer to the legal file drawer. It was open: flipping on a small beam flashlight and perusing through the files and finding that Boxer hadn't changed the names of anything. He almost thanked Boxer for overlooking that. Plugging the five different thumb drives into a small download memory device, then quickly putting everything back into the pouch and closed the file. Next it was on too Boxers office where he hoped he would find the real prize.

Again he wondered, with all the electronic secure devices on all the doors and windows, then why is there always a ladder somewhere around the office. Finding that, he removed a ceiling tile then setting the stick for one pound over, he lightly floated into and through the suspended ceiling. If anything, he had to push off the sub-floor above sometimes to keep moving.

"The only way to travel! Ha ha."
Repeating the dropping into the office space maneuver, he quickly repeated the same steps as before. Attaching the search code device to the desk legal file drawer. While that was finding the sequence, he wasn't sure if there was a safe somewhere, moving purposely to look through the bookcase then behind the wall hangings. Nothing, ok back to the file cabinet and again finding labeled mini drives,

"Hum, easy thanks."

Now with that done, he looked around for something to stand on to get back up in the ceiling. Nothing, now he thought if one pound = six inches how about two pounds, trying that he did lift off one foot. So he added six pounds and turning it on with a small push-off he found he had launched himself through the ceiling and smashing into the concrete subfloor above!

"Now I'm the dumb shit, ouch!" Thinking: sorry Auch not you.

Fitting the ceiling tile back into place and moving back to the ladder, now doing everything in reverse. Back at Sophie's old desk, he reset the gravity stick for five pounds over and gently pushed off. As he was pulling his feet up, the lights came on everywhere! Instinctively he carried on with his escape, and just as instinctively the security people started to yell,

"Stop where you are, stop where you are, we will shoot!" Carter had no intention to do as requested, moving on into the drop ceiling space, he was thinking of the floor plan of the office and how he would exit. It was at that point that seven different types of weapons started shooting through the ceiling randomly. He could tell by all the different holes the light was sifting up through on each pattern.

As he floated between ceiling and subfloor above, he muttered a short prayer,

"God please make this work."
Watching in slow motion as the bullets made their way towards him, he closed his eyes and cringed. The next second he opened his eyes to see the swarm of bullets cut right below him, nothing, he felt nothing. Next thought was; 'am I dead?' next thought: nope, cause I can see the bullet lights in the ceiling passing me. In a little in shock, he waited for some seconds. They were yelling something and then the gun fire stopped.

"Hay shut the fuck up!! Stop shooting assholes!"
Of course that took a while,

"I said stop shit heads!"
The lead man yelled out,

"Look for blood."
A quick survey found nothing: so what else do you do? You start shooting more.   They were having such a nice time, changing out their clips for the larger capacity ammo clips with smiles on their faces.

While the shooting gallery was in full operation, Carter had decided on a path back to the supply closet out in the reception area. As he floated by all the AC duct work moving along the 75 or 80 feet away from all the noise, he keep thinking to himself,

"Why didn't I think of this earlier…easier this!"
Knowing that there wouldn't be any of the private guards in their right minds standing around watching the front door with all the noise back there, and he was right! They didn't want to miss a chance to shoot their guns at a live target. Carter wanting to be careful, set the ladder back on its rack and resetting the g-stick for his regular weight, he carefully opened the door. They hadn't bothered to turn any lights on out in the reception area when they snuck in, they were still too busy shooting at the ceiling. By now they had hit a couple of fire sprinkler heads and water was going in every direction. Still some of the faithful were still shooting at shadows.

Carter, walking through the dark parking lot was little too casual, he came face to face with a 9mm pointed right at his head,

"Don't move, you do your dead."

So what's the first thing Carter do: he moves toward the man, the
man fires once thinking that should do it at this close range. As
he moved forward, pulled the gravity-stick out and swung hard.
There was three more aloud noises; one was the gun going off,
one ricocheting off Carters head, the other was the man's jaw
cracking. In the dim-black of the night, Carter didn't wait around
to do any more damage, quietly moving off and was back at his
car a few blocks away. He started laughing about the bullet
ridden office driving back to his place thinking: I can't wait to tell
Sophie about all the remodeling at her old office!

Chapter 46

San Diego was a nice place to be on a Saturday. Particularly sitting in a sand chair on the bayside of south mission beach with a pastrami sammy & beer, with a bunch of friends.

Alouette "You know, we live right here, and we don't do this enough! What's wrong with us!"

Perla "I agree you should invite us down more often; don't you agree Richard?"

"I think I'm saposta say 'yes dear.' But wouldn't that be doubly rude if we invite ourselves twice to come again to your way cool place?"

Alouette "Let me help; you two are welcome any time you like. There, now that's out of the way, after we finish lunch let's all go on a bike ride down to the jetty and back."

Wyatt "Then it's nap time!"

Everybody had a small laugh, but each one was thinking that would be really nice to throw a blanket out with some sun block on and hug the warm sand for a while.

They did take a nice bike ride but came in and started talking about court things here on Earth.

Wyatt "What we don't want is this to get thrown out into the 'National Security' ozone, there, nobody hears about any of this. I wonder if we could ask some of whoever gets nominated to visit the Earth in a couple of weeks too help. Or if they can, I am hoping that we can get some leverage with the group visiting here."

Alouette "You mean have them all here here! You'd have to close off accesses to South Mission at the roily-coaster!"

Wyatt "Ha, not here here, over in the desert. That way we could land a couple of ships and only a few of our neighbors might notice, maybe."

Richard "I'll ask Auch an see if he could recommend something. How about landing them over at Sophie's place and take them on a bus tour of Washington DC?"

Alouette "I think that might have more of an impact than the desert. They mostly come from places that resembles the desert like the Moon or Alpha Centauri, or Zeta Reticula or Proxima C. DC might really hold their interest."

The talk continued on into the early afternoon, still trying to land on the perfect idea to let the world know about their Space neighbors.

A thought passed Perla,

"You know, what if you guys drop the idea of introducing our neighbors via the courts, and maybe head up to New York and just drop in on the United Nations with the Moon group. It might seem a little friendlier. I mean, just to get the negative court feeling away from the idea being introduced to the general populist. What do ya think?"

That did stop everyone enough to really reconsider their one true goal, and that was a comfortable friendly introduction of our neighbors.

Al "You are absolutely right. I think we should move away from any 'Law' issues and take up the friendly ones."

Wyatt "I think you two are on to a better line of introduction and I think now we have enough sway with the Judge. I know

Auch turned things around for us, so to speak. We could easily settle and move on, Perla you are right.
 We need 'friendly feelings' and less 'law,' so I'll call the attorneys now and leave a message to move in that direction."

Chapter 47

The Pentagon was having quiet a few issues with Mr. Boxer and his way of doing business.

"Your budget has tripled! You no longer have access to the Moon! We don't have any reliable information on the now six individuals that have taken over your role on the Moon!"

Boxer "Well, now you see how much work it is! I was doing everything myself and now it takes six people!"

"Boxer, you small minded door stop! Stop sounding like the idiot moron over in the White House who imagines he knows how to brush his teeth!! That idiot at least would… now that I think about it, he is in the same class as you! He doesn't know how to do anything!!"

Boxer "I'll get results, I'll have them taken out quietly or…"

"You fucking lunatic. You let them become Ambassadors up there so now they have a safety with the people that would bring the power of the Moon down on us right here!!"

This went back and forth for about five more minutes, but the General already was convinced he was right with his forgone conclusion.

"We will no longer need any of your services. Remove your personal things from your office and I never want to see you again!!"

He actually started crying, thinking this worked for the guy that was going for the Supreme Court 2018.

"Cut that crybaby sit out! that only works for rich republicans dumbshit assholes who are connected with the stupidest president this country has ever had. Get the Hell out!!"

Leaving the office the secretary pool was quietly listening in on the intercom and were watching with sideways glances and smirk's on their faces. Moving quickly through the long hallways out of the building, in his car he called his lieutenant.

"Ok that went just like I wanted, now let's get my own E.T. response team going…"

Very delighted with himself he moved off to the airport, getting on his jet and heading for Texas with a bucket tumbler of vodka in one hand and the phone in the other.

Chapter 48

A very happy group of three stepped out of floating craft in the dark of the Borrego night too be greeted by another group of four.

Wyatt "Come on in you guys, Auch do we have a few minutes?"

"Yes of course, what do you propose?"

"A toast to new interstellar relations and attorneys in the rearview mirror!"

Alouette had a nice small dessert island set with all kinds of different mini servings of ice cream & fruit. It was very nice for thirty minutes but then Auch had to gather the group,

"I would like to invite you all to my apartment where my wife has much of the same already. Shall we?"

Sophie "How fun! A wandering traveling party that ends up on the Moon! Boy if I put that on an invitation, we would have the world beating a path to our doors!"

Everybody stopped what they were doing and looked at Sophie...

Richard "That's it!!"

Carter "That is it!

Wyatt "Auch do you think we could pull something like that off?"

"Of course there could be arrangement's made for a medium number of people. It would certainly give the cause something to aspire too."

Alouette "That also would open the tourist option wide open! People would naturally want to know why we have been using rockets and jets for any kind of travel.

The public would demand gravity deafferentation!"

Wyatt "Aum, I don't think my Dad would approve of that word…"

Alouette looking up, "Sorry Dad, I just made it up!"

Auch "Shall we head for the Moon?"

Everybody en mass,

"YES, Let's go!!!"

Epilogue

All things now had a reason, a purpose with a very attractive goal for the world in general. All of the straggling loose ends were starting to tie together in a comfortable way.

Boxer had a different plan for the world entirely, nothing short of direct outright invasion of the Moon was all over his agenda and all of the militia that he had amassed with him.

ABOUT THE AUTHOR

Born and raised in San Diego, as the youngest member of a Pastor's family, an older brother and my tireless Mother. We as a family, were able to live in Coalsnaughton, a village in Clackmannanshire, Scotland north of Sterling for a long summer.

I was at the age of twelve and fell in with the village boys/girls making mischief with all the beautiful countryside had to offer.

Subsequently, another extended holiday visiting notable people, and interlacing places all through Europe.

Not finishing College, the lure of tangible's took me into a G-Construction license.

Married and was blessed with Triplet Girls,

who now are about to finish what their Father didn't.

My out of door actives took-in a wide spray

of Surfing, Skiing, Moto-cross, Flying, Rock climbing, Trekking, and Diving.

I can't go anywhere without mentioning my

lifelong Family of friends, they are responsible for helping me through my Sixty-five years.

Presently single, thankfully retired and thriving in Hawaii.

ALSO, by JON W. SHAW

Annotated Notes in Time:

Book 1.   EARTHS - Invisible Presence©

Book 2.   LINGERING EARTHS -
A Precipitous Presence©

Book 3.   ENDURING EARTHS –
A Propitious Presence©

And

STEMMING TROUBLE©
Adventure

In A Blue Moon©
Adventure

210

Due 2021:

<u>Serendipity</u>

Growing up

Made in the USA
Columbia, SC
23 October 2020